Nicholas Rescher
Is Philosophy Dispensable?
And Other Philosophical Essays

Nicholas Rescher

Is Philosophy Dispensable?

And Other Philosophical Essays

ontos
verlag

Frankfurt I Paris I Ebikon I Lancaster I New Brunswick

Bibliographic information published by Deutsche Nationalbibliothek
The Deutsche Nationalbibliothek lists this publication in the Deutsche Nationalbibliographie;
detailed bibliographic data is available in the Internet at http://dnb.ddb.de

North and South America by
Transaction Books
Rutgers University
Piscataway, NJ 08854-8042
trans@transactionpub.com

United Kingdom, Eire, Iceland, Turkey, Malta, Portugal by
Gazelle Books Services Limited
White Cross Mills
Hightown
LANCASTER, LA1 4XS
sales@gazellebooks.co.uk

Livraison pour la France et la Belgique:
Librairie Philosophique J.Vrin
6, place de la Sorbonne; F-75005 PARIS
Tel. +33 (0)1 43 54 03 47; Fax +33 (0)1 43 54 48 18
www.vrin.fr

©2007 ontos verlag
P.O. Box 15 41, D-63133 Heusenstamm
www.ontosverlag.com

ISBN 978-3-938793-45-9

2007

Printed on acid-free paper
FSC-certified (Forest Stewardship Council)
This hardcover binding meets the International Library standard

Printed in Germany
by buch bücher **dd ag**

For Mario Bunge

Scientist, Philosopher, and Friend

Is Philosophy Dispensable?
And Other Philosophical Essays

Contents

PREFACE

During 2005-2006 I continued my longstanding practice of writing occasional studies on philosophical topics, both for formal presentation and for informal discussion with colleagues. While my forays of this kind have usually issued in journal publications, this has not been so in the preset case so that the studies offered here encompass substantially new material. Notwithstanding their thematic variation, they manifest a uniformity of treatment and method in a way that is characteristic of my philosophical modus operandi and inherent in its endeavors to treat classical issues from novel points of view.

Nicholas Rescher
Pittsburgh PA
August 2006

Chapter 1

IS PHILOSOPHY DISPENSABLE? (AN APORETIC ANALYSIS)

It is one of the ironies of 20th century philosophy that a self-loathing of sorts pervades the enterprise. The era's schools of thought of otherwise the most varied and reciprocally discordant views seem to agree on one— and perhaps only one—significant point: that the discipline as traditionally understood and historically cultivated is misguided, profoundly wrong, and in crying need of abandonment. With remarkable unanimity, the philosophers of the 20th century have wanted to replace philosophy as traditionally practiced by something else. Science, logic, linguistics of some sort, history of ideas, sociology, and cultural studies have all figured among one theorist or another's favored successors. Virtually no one has been content to see philosophy do business as usual.

In the century's course this sort of anti-philosophical view has become pervasive. Martin Heidegger spoke disdainfully of traditional metaphysics as "a mere vestige of Christian theology". And we find comparably dismissive postures in logical positivism, in Wittgenstein, in various versions of pragmatism, in analytic and especially in ordinary language philosophy, in Karl Marx's insistence that while philosophy's historic mission has been to understand the world the real task is to change it. And then too there is the so-called quietism of Wittgenstein-inspired philosophers such as Cora Diamond and John McDowell.[1]

As an incidental aside it deserves remark that the term *quietism* is a singularly unfortunate choice for the skeptical position at issue, given the established usage of that expression. Here is what the Humanities Press *Dictionary of Philosophy and Religion* has to say about what quietism involves:

[Quietism is] A 17th-century devotional and mystical movement within the Catholic Church ... The movement held that the path to the discovery of the divine will require one to "sell or kill" one's self-conscious will. One's whole soul may thus be directed to the love of God. Waiting on God, meditation became central. A quietist maxim held that one moment's contemplation is worth a thousand years good works.[2]

Now whatever the antiphilosophical position of those latter-day so-called quietists may have in mind, it is surely not a matter of prioritizing contemplative meditation over good works.

But issues of terminology aside, the problem with the dismissive treatment of philosophy is that it fails to do justice to the consideration that philosophizing is effectively indispensable within the broader context of rational inquiry. And the point at issue here is perhaps most persuasively made obliquely—through concrete examples rather than directly through the general principles they instantiate.

So let us begin with an example from epistemology. Consider the following three contentions:

(1) Claims to factual knowledge are sometimes rationally appropriate.

(2) For rational appropriateness, the specifics of factual knowledge must always be certain. (It makes no sense to say "I know that p is the case, but there is some shadow of doubt about it [or: it may fail to be so].")

(3) Claims to absolute, indubitable certainty are never rationally appropriate.

The trouble with this trio is that its contentions are logically inconsistent. Mere rationality accordingly demands that least one or the other of its contentions must be rejected. And no matter which way we turn we will become enmeshed in a venture of substantive philosophizing. For in rejecting such a thesis as nonconceptable we effectively ally ourselves to its negation. And so consider:

(1)-rejection. Claims to factual knowledge are never rationally appropriate. (Scepticism.)

(2)-rejection. Factual knowledge need not be certain. (Cognitive fallibilism.)

(3)-rejection. Claims to absolute and indubitable certainty are sometimes appropriate. (Cataleptic Evidentism.)

In every and any case we are in effect caught up within the domain of one or another tried and true philosophical position.

And this sort of thing is quite general. Thus consider the following group of contentions:

(1) All occurrences in nature, human acts included, are causally determined.

(2) Humans can and do act freely on occasion.

(3) A genuinely free act cannot be causally determined—for if it were so determined, then the act would not be free by virtue of this very circumstance.

What we have here is an inconsistent group whose resolution is open to various alternatives:

(1)-rejection. A "voluntaristic" exemption of free acts for the web of causal determination. (Descartes)

(2)-rejection. A "deterministic" subjection of the will to causal constraints. (Spinoza)

(3)-rejection. A "compatibilism" of free action and causal determination—for example via a theory that distinguishes between inner and outer causal determination, and sees the former sort as compatible with freedom. (Leibniz)

Of course, while one or the other of those rejections is mandatory, there remains a wide latitude of options with respect to the rationale through which this step is going to be accounted for. (Those philosopher-indicated philosophical positions are mere examples of the sort of story that could be told here.) But the key fact remains that no matter what sort of account one is prepared to give, the story being told will be told in the way of philosophy. Whatever sort of rationale we offer for that rejection is going to be philosophical in its nature and bearing.

Or again, consider yet another example:

(1) Acting unjustly is always impermissible.

(2) In some—inherently dilemmatic—circumstances an unjust action is unavoidable.

(3) An act that is unavoidable (in the circumstances) cannot be impermissible (in those circumstances).

Here too we have an inconsistent triad. A rational person cannot but abandon one or the other of them. But in view of his supposed rationality, our rejector will be committed to acting for a reason. His very rationality binds him to having some sort of rationale for his proceeding. And once the rejector offers an explanatory rationale for this rejection he is doing philosophy.

Thus for example we might have the following situation:

(1)-rejection. Acting unjustly is sometimes permissible. For the least of evils is always permissible and in suitably unfortunate circumstances this least of evils can involve some element of injustice.

(2)-rejection. The realizability of just action is never unavailable. For the best available alternative for acting can never count as unjust.

(3)-rejection. An act that is unavoidable can indeed be impermissible. For there can be moral dilemmas that force a choice between impermissible acts.

And in each case, the rationale at issue provides for an enmeshment in what cannot but count as a philosophical position.

So here is the situation. For starters, we are confronted with a group of collectively incompatible propositions. And these propositions can be devoid of any transparent philosophical involvement. But given their collective inconsistency one or the other of them has to go. And providing a plausible rationale for the specific rejection of any particular one of them is inevitably going to involve us in philosophical deliberations of the sort that are quintessentially philosophical.

To be sure, faced with the imperative of rejection in such cases, a theorist may go all-out and take the following line:

—I shall never accept anything because no contention is ever acceptable. (Scepticism)

or perhaps somewhat more restrictedly:

—I shall never accept anything that has any bearing on philosophical matters. (Since virtually every fact has some degree of philosophical relevancy, this sort of scepticism has a tendency to transmute into the preceding, seemingly more radical sort.)

Now when any position along such lines is rendered rational by being fitted out with a plausible rationale of some sort, then we at once find ourselves back at philosophizing—deeply engaged in the epistemology of rational acceptance. And we then face the problem that the sort of broadcast approach represented by that envisioned reaction is not really appropriate because the rejection of *specific* contentions of the sort at issue in our apories calls for the deployment of case-specific consideration. In matters of specific rejection a wholesale approach through guilt by association will hardly be justifiable. Our skeptical anti-philosopher effectively says:

A plague in all your houses. The very philosophical bearing (oblique or otherwise) that those inconsistent clusters involve brings all of these conflicting theses within the scope of my antiphilosophical proscription. I thus reject the whole lot of them without further ado or scrutiny. I see no reason to confront them individually in their idiosyncratic detail.

However, this plausible-seeming stance fails to meet the needs of the situation. For the very dialectic of rational controversy precludes this tactic. Consider an illustration. You say: "All Cretans are liars." I present you with a particular Cretan and say: "This man is no liar." There is now no longer any option but to look into the mouth of this particular gift horse. It will no longer do to remain at the level of wholesale generality and say: "But he is a Cretan and all Cretans are liars." For it is exactly this sort of generalization that is in question.

The fact of it is that the dialectic of rational controversy prioritizes specifics over generalities.[3] In this sort of situation presumption stands on the side of the particular and the burden of proof rests on the side of generality. So the anti-philosopher has no viable excuse for refusing to engage the details of particular cases.

The overall lesson is as follows: If you are going to be rational then you are bound to confront some contentions which you cannot but reject, and which are such that the moment you try to provide *grounds* for this rejection and set out some sort of *rationale* for it, then—like it or not—you are going to be involved in philosophizing. Philosophy, that is to say, is effectively unavoidable in the rational scheme of things.

There is, of course, the theoretical possibility of taking the stance that was indeed taken by some of the leading skeptics of classical antiquity, namely that of living *adoxastos* (without doctrine), going along in life doing all sorts of things without worrying about the rhyme or reason of it following the drift of inclination, habit, or custom. Effectively, one says: "I have better things to do than to concern myself about reasons for what I do or think." This is no doubt a stance one can indeed take, and there are doubtless many people who take it. But it is clear that such an abandonment of reason is not a stance that is *rationally* defensible. It is not that people cannot refrain from philosophizing, but rather that rational people have no cogent rationale from urging its abandonment.

NOTES FOR CHAPTER 1

[1] The use of the term quietism to characterize Wittgenstein's anti-philosophical position apparently became current in Oxford during the 1970s with such philosophers as Crispin Wright, Simon Blackburn, and Nick Zangwill. It has been enroute to transmutation from Wittgenstein exegesis to outright advocacy in such neo-Wittgensteinean philosophers as Cora Diamond and John McDowell. See David G. Stern, *Wittgenstein's Philosophical Investigations* (Cambridge: Cambridge University Press, 2004), pp. 168-70.

[2] *Dictionary of Philosophy and Religion*, ed. by W. L. Reese (Atlantic Highlands, NJ: Humanities Press, 1980), p. 628.

[3] This theme is developed at some length in the author's book *Conditionals* (Cambridge, Mass: MIT Press, 2007).

Chapter 2

FIRST PRINCIPLES AND THEIR PLACE IN PHILOSOPHY

1. ALTERNATIVE APPROACHES TO FIRST PRINCIPLES: AN APORETIC SURVEY

Since scholastic times, philosophical deliberations have traditionally dealt with first principles under two headings: first principles of being (*principia essendi*) and first principles of knowing (*principia cognoscendi*). The former are those that relate to existence and coming to be.[1] But it is the latter alone—the basic principles of cognition—that will concern the present discussion.

There are of course many different modes of firstness. (After all, the expression "first lady of the land" does not necessarily stand for the original founding mother.) Principles can be cognitively first in point of systemic fundamentality, in point of importance, in point of range of application, and doubtless in various other respects as well. But it is the first of these, systemic fundamentality in the order of rational exposition, that will be at the focus of the present deliberations, and it is specifically the fundamentality oriented sense of the expression, and this alone, that will figure in the preset discussion.

In rational deliberation we substantiate our claims by providing reasons, that is to say, with arguments. But arguments have premises and these too must establish their credentials. Yet if the process is not to go on *ad infinitum*, it must—seemingly—have a stop with basic "first principles" of some sort that are ultimate in the order of exposition. Accordingly, the idea of and the demand for "first principles" arises from a seemingly straightforward line of thought:

Cognitive rationality demands that there always should be a rationale for the contentions to which we commit ourselves. But this immediately poses the problem of an infinite regress, confronting us with the spectre of an unending series of childhood-reminiscent "Why?"-questions. The only way out of this difficulty is by endorsing the idea of first principles—truths that are basic to inquiry and are evident truths which as such can dispense with any further external support.

From this point of departure there has emerged a series of distinct positions on this issue which can be viewed as emanating from the following group of thesis:

(1) Rational cognition is possible: some facts can be known with rational cogency.

(2) Rational cogency requires first principles able to provide ultimate grounding for acceptable theses.

[3] There indeed are rationally cogent first principles, capable of providing for the rational grounding of acceptable theses. [From (1) and (2).]

(4) The rational acceptability of these first principles must itself be grounded somehow. Some viable rationale must speak for their endorsement: they must have some sort of substantiating basis.

(5) There are only two pathways to rational grounding: the experientially immediate and the deliberative discursive.

(6) Experience cannot ground first principles. In view of their inherent generality, there is no sure-fire way for principles to be experientially evident. Every experiential mode of thesis-establishment can malfunction.

(7) Discursive reasoning cannot ground first principles. First principles cannot—by nature of their very fabric—be established by any deliberative consideration.

[8] There just is no rationally cogent way of grounding first principles: No such principles are rationally available. (From (5), (6), (7).)

(9) [8] contradicts [3].

This group constitutes an *apory* or *aporetic cluster* of collectively inconsistent but seemingly plausible theses. In this family as in so many others irreconcilable differences arise. In matters of theory rather than real-life, such conflicts must be resolved by ejection—that is to say by their abandonment.

In the present circumstances there are only six exits for this apory, viz. the rejection of one or more of the six theses: (1), (2), (4), (5), (6), (7). Let us look at them.

(1)-rejection (Skepticism)

This is no more (or less) than radical skepticism.

(2)-rejection (Catateptic Evidentism)

Perhaps theses could be validated without principles by a direct insight along the lines of Descartes' "clear and distinct perceptions of the mind" which certified facts without further principled ado. Or again, think of the cataleptics perception of the Stoics.

(4)-rejection (Self-evidentism)

First principles do not require a guiding rationale. They are self-evident.

(5)-rejection (Processism)

Further modes of grounding might possibly be on offer—a principle-dismissive reliabilism, for example, which guides theses via their sources or discovery processes.

(6)-rejection (Platonic Intuitionism)

There are two possible alternatives here. The idea of failproof episodic experience (as per the Stoic or Cartesian certitude) is once more available that of an intuition-based Platonism of some sort) is yet another possibility.

(7)-rejection (Importationism Cohentism)

There are two possibilities here: (1) the idea of importing principles ab extra—from other domains (as in Aristotle), or (2) the idea of a intrasystemic, "in the end" substantiation (as with per coherentist pragmatism).

Given the inconsistency at issue in the aporetic cluster under consideration, one or more of these alternatives has to be adopted. The range of rationally viable options is limited. Only so many approaches to first principles are available. Let us look at them in yet greater detail.

2. DIFFERENT MODES OF FIRST PRINCIPLES

A. *First Principles as Evident* (Catateptic Evidentism)

Since (by definition) first principles are not established discursively by some sort of inference from previously accessible cognitive material and are unmediated by derivation from more fundamental theses, they may well grounded directly in experience of some sort—evoked immediately by reality's impact on the cognitive facilities of man. They are (in some Cartesian sense) the product of "clear and distinct perceptions of the mind"—the product of an insight analogous to, though decidedly distinct from, sensory perception. They root in mental insight rather than sensory sight and it is the systemic operation of our minds rather than that of our senses which—in appropriate circumstances—reveals them to our awareness. They can accordingly "dawn upon us" by a process which is complex and systemic; in contrast to sense perception which is experiential in an *episodic* mode. Such cognitive insight can develop over the longer term in response to a *course* of experience, the product of *Erfahrung* rather than *Erlebnis* to revoke the German distinction between systemic and episodic experience.

B. *First Principles as Self-Evident* (Self-Evidentism)

Another cognitive pathway to the realization of first principles is provided by the idea of the "self-evident". Experiencing the fact at issue by way of its recognition and entertainment is of itself acceptance-compelling. The cogency of such principles speaks for itself—they wear their obvious acceptability on their own sleeves. Consider "Equals added to equals yield equals" or "Some changes can occur faster than others". These are not substantial discoveries. No-one will earn a prize for this sort of thing—the facts at issue are obvious, trivial, truistic. They are evident on the very face of it—self-evident by virtue of their transparent cogency.

C. *First Principles as Domain Relative* (Domain Relativism/Imputationism)

Principles be they first or last have to be about something. They have a subject—matter environment; they belong to some division of discourse; they form part of some field of inquiry or deliberation. On this basis, the fundamentality of firstness can be something that is only domain-relative. To take Aristotle's example, the physical does not deliberate the desirability of health—it is a given of the field. Nor does the arithmetician question the excellence of quantities—it is a presupposed given of his field. The "first principle" of one domain may thus be one that is simply taken from another. And for any such principle of a given domain there will be some other domain in which it is somehow or other established.

Firstness is accordingly seen as context relative rather than absolute and unconditioned. The question "But just where do those first principles come from?" is systemically answered: Elsewhere! And the question "What is it that provides for *this* grounding?" is systematically answered: "That's not our problem—it is the problem of some other domain, viz. that which constitutes this domain of origin—a matter quite outside the range of our concerns." Thus the first principles of cookery may (for example) find their natural homeland in the field of organic chemistry, but this is something which, as such, simply does not concern cooks.

D. *First Principles as Final*

D₁: Coherentism

A coherentist view of first principles refuses to accord them any sort of inaugurating or foundational role. In the first instance this fundamentality is not absolute but provisional. Instead coherentism sees the development of knowledge setting out for a basis of highly provisional, tentative presumptive information and sees that epistemic task as a mode of striving for an optimally harmonious supplementization of this body of material which will revise, qualify emend or even simply discord its membership in the interests of optimal systematization. The implementization at issue would thus be seen as a matter of *cognitive upgrading* in the status of a claim through a sequential process, as per: tentative (provisional) $\Rightarrow$ systemic integration $\Rightarrow$ systemic confirmation. (It is like working out a jigsaw puzzle with extra pieces.) Those so-called "first principles" are the theses which emerge as paramount at the end of the systematizing processes, being called upon to play a basic axiomatic role in the finality realized systematization of this material. They are regarded as "basic" to a rational inquiry alright, but emerge as such not at the start but only at the end of the process of inquiry and systematization. Though first in the order of fundamentality they are last in the order of learning emerging as first principles in the retrospective contemplation of an entire course of experience involving the developed systematization of an entire body of knowledge.

D_2: Pragmatism

Instead if basing acceptance in such theoretical considerations of substantiating grounding one proceeds wholly on the basis of a pragmatic empiricism of trial and error—one doesn't "buy in on" theses straight off but "test drives" then, so to speak, by way of provisional adoption as a basis for trial and error implementation. Optimally, this process could not be applied to inductive theses at all, but rather to methods or processes for their endorsement. Rational acceptance is thus seen not as a matter of evidentiation of some sort (be it episodic or systemic) but entirely on the basis of performance. Retrospective efficacy in application becomes the crux.

E. *First Principles as Dispensable* (Processism)

There remains yet another sort of approach—one that dismisses first principles altogether and looks for its fundamentals not to principles at all but methods or processes or procedures for establishing theses. Validation is not achieved through inference or reasoning from something more fundamental but rather issues directly from that process/procedure/method which figures as an immediate source of information. Thus to authenticate *memory* (for example) as a reliable facility takes reasoning but that does not mean that any reasoning is involved when memory itself attests to something. Thanks to its focus on the reliability of certain processes or procedures, this sort of approach is often characterized as Reliabilism. Its crux is that what is now at issue is not a fundamental premise or group thereof, but rather a premiss-generating process or procedure or proven effectiveness.

So much then for the spectrum of generally available positions with respect to first principles. As expected, we find there to be a limited range of available alternatives.

3. CLASSICAL THEORIES OF FIRST PRINCIPLES

It is instructive to survey the historical situation regarding first principles, seeing that the history of the subject has pretty well canvassed the spectrum of available possibilities.

PLATO

The basic idea at issue with first principles goes back to the very dawn of speculative thought about the nature of explanation—to Plato's discussion in the *Republic* (at Book VII, 510 BC).

In studying geometric matters, the mind is compelled to employ assumptions, and, because it cannot rise above these, does not travel upwards to a first principle; and moreover the mind here uses diagrams as images of those actual things. However, this mathematical domain contrasts with the [philosophical] domain of the intelligible world which unaided reasoning apprehends by the power of dialectic. This treats its assumptions, not as first principles, but as *hypotheses* in the literal sense, things "laid down" like a flight of steps up which it may mount all the way to something that is not hypothetical, the first principle of all. Then, having grasped this, the mind may turn back and, holding on to the consequences which depend upon it, descend at last to a conclusion, never making use of any sensible object, but only of Forms, moving through Forms from one to another, and ending with Forms. [And so we must] distinguished the field of intelligible reality studied by dialectic as having a greater certainty and truth than the subject-matter of the 'arts', as they are called, which treat their assumptions as first principles. The students of these arts are, it is true, compelled to exercise thought in contemplating objects which the senses cannot perceive; but because they start from assumptions without going back to a first principle, you do not regard them as gaining true understanding about those objects, although the objects themselves, when connected with a first principle, are intelligible.

As such deliberations indicate, Plato—the first of many—found the idea of unexplained explainers unpalatable. His complaint regarding Euclidean style geometry, for example, is just exactly this—that it proceeds from first principles that are laid down as arbitrary stipulations ("absolute hypotheses") and not themselves fitted out with an explanatory rationale. As Plato saw it, even with mathematical truths proof as such is not of itself sufficient. Mathematics alone, he holds, can yield certain knowledge independently of experience. But what is its basis? Proof—deductive demonstration—does no more than to trace validation back to the first principles—to the axioms, possibilities, and definition. But what is it that justifies these?—so Plato asks in book VII of the *Republic*. And his answer is effectively this: that while theses are usually justified by retrospection, by deduction from first principles,[2] these first principles themselves are validated nor deductively by demonstration from something yet more basic, but rather by dialectic, by pro-spection, by looking forward towards the overall system of established results. And while the deduction of a theorem is always a finite process of a number of discrete steps, the latter, the dialectical utility of axioms and first principles in their wider rational context, is essentially an unending process of looking forward towards the overall merit of the entire system that results.

By contrast, the great merit of philosophy—as he saw it—is that it treats its first principles not as absolute but as provisional hypotheses and that it proceeds not *deductively* but *dialectically*, looking backwards along the chain of consequences in order to substantiate the principle from which they derived their credibility. With regard to mathematical first principles Plato is in effect a coherentist.

Overall, Plato's position stressed the idea that for thoroughgoing rationality one must take the dialectical approach of justifying one's beliefs cyclically, so to speak, by looking initially to self-recommending first principles which themselves are then subsequent evaluated with reference to their consequences and ramifications. As Plato thus saw it, the standard process of mathematical justification of terms of absolute hypotheses that themselves remain unjustified—however customary in geometry or arithmetic—is ultimately unsatisfactory from a rational point of view because it leaves off at the point where a different, dialectical methodology is called for.

And Plato carries this line of thought further in the *Timaeus* by shifting matters from mathematics to natural philosophy. Here too fitness—value, systemic order, harmonious coordination—is once more the governing standard—only now for the arrangements of nature rather than in the realm of mathematical abstraction. Our understanding of nature must be predicated on "the principle that this universe was fashioned from the beginning by the victory of reasonable persuasion [i.e., lawful order] over mere force [i.e., necessity] [as it is here in the fortuitous machinations of brute matter]."[3] For Plato then the ultimate arbiter of truth—as in mathematics and natural philosophy alike—is fitness, harmony, rational coordination, systemic order. And so for Plato, paradoxical though it may seem, the determination of what is basic in philosophy does not come at the start of an inquiry but at its end.

Here, at the level of fundamentals, it is systemic fitness that is the deciding factor. Merit, rational order—the Platonic conception of "the Good"—becomes the supreme arbiter. And so with respect to first principles Plato was effectively a coherentist.

ARISTOTLE

Aristotle maintained that a science is defined as the discipline it is by the manifold of its characteristics problems, and that its first principles are those theses that must be accepted if those problems are to be meaningfully and cogently addressed.[4] We thus cannot expect to realize an answer (let alone substantiate the answer) to a scientific problem if we fail to accept the first principles of the science at issue.

Overall, Aristotle holds a complex position with regard to first principles. (1) The characteristic first principles of special sciences come either on loan from *other* special sciences, or from experience via intuition, or from dialectical analysis of commonalities among the such relevant theory (*endoxa*). And (2) the characteristic first principles of general science (logic and metaphysics) are based on a dialectical analysis of the sine qua non requisites of rational thought and discourse.[5]

In the *Posterior Analytics* (72a14-24), where Aristotle has in view the role of "Euclidean" geometry as a paradigm science, he divides first principles into theses and axioms, the former being in turn divided into hypotheses and stipulations (*horismoi*). However, in metaphysics, the science of being qua being, the only first principles are axioms—there is no place for hypotheses or stipulations, these being encountered in its special science alone. Accordingly, as Aristotle sees it, the first principles of universal science are those rules which—like the avoidance of selfcontradiction—are determinative for meaning and meaningfulness at large while in the special sense they will also include the stipulative specifications that characterize the range of issues definitive of the particular science at hand.[6]

And so Aristotle effectively adopted versions of different approaches with respect to different issues: Domain Relativism with regard to the special sciences; Self-evidentism in matters of general science (metaphysics as the science of being qua being); Processism with regard to our nature-endowed cognitive faculties (sense and memory); and finally, a Coherentism of sorts in relation to our ordinary knowledge of everyday common-sense matters.

THE STOICS

The Stoics held that the first principles of factual knowledge issue from particularly clear and telling "cataleptic perceptions"—from truth-certifying experience of a certain sort. They regarded the normal everyday judgments of sensory experience under favorable conditions as paradigmatic, with illusion and delusions dismissed as aberrant abnormalities. And they also credited the human mind with an analogous insight, with the basic judgments of simple mathematics, for example, being secured along comparable lines.

AQUINAS

Aristotle set the stage of medieval philosophizing, and throughout the Aristotelian tradition, first principles of knowledge function to countervail the idea that demonstration requires demonstrable premises via the availability of theses known non-inferentially as a matter of immediate insight via their "evident" or "self-evident" nature.[7] The Aristotelism of the middle ages accordingly emphasized in particular the Self-evidentism adopted by the master himself in relation to matters of metaphysics. And so Aquinas, along with much of the subsequent neo-Aristotelian tradition, endorsed the idea of an "immediate" (inferentially unmediated knowledge of the fundamentals that are evident in the very nature of things in themselves—*per ipsas*).[8] Principles thus become cognitively available through a suitable course of experience and perceived faithfully ("clearly and distinctly" in Cartesian terminology) by an attentive reason.[9]

DESCARTES

Descartes has it that the first principles of knowledge come from "clear and distinct perceptions of the mind", as provided by the human intellect's divinity endowed capacity for the immediate apprehension of basic truth. On this effectively Evidentist approach, knowledge of first principles thus emerges from the exercise of a particular (God-given) capacity for intellectual insight.

LEIBNIZ

For Leibniz, the first principles of factual (phenomical) knowledge are rooted in cognitive systematization.

Leibniz treats this epistemological issue in one of his most powerfully seminal works, the little tract *De modo distinguendi phaenomena realia ab imaginariis*. How does the golden mountain I imagine differ from the real earthern, rocky, and wooden mountain I see yonder? Primarily in two respects: internal detail and general conformity to the course of nature. Regarding the internal detail of vividness and complexity Leibniz says:

> We conclude it from the phenomenon itself if it is vivid, complex, and internally coherent [*congruum*]. It will be vivid if its qualities, such as light, color, and warmth, appear intense enough. It will be complex if these qualities are varied and support us in undertaking many experiments and new observations; for example, if we experience in a phenomenon not merely colors but also sounds, odors, and qualities of taste and touch, and this both in the phenomenon as a whole and in its various parts which we can further treat according to causes. Such a long chain of observations is usually begun by design and selectively and usually occurs neither in dreams nor in those imaginings which memory or fantasy present, in which the image is mostly vague and disappears while we are examining it.[10]

And as regards coherence, the second key aspect of cognitive reason, Leibniz says:

> A phenomenon will be coherent when it consists of many phenomena, for which a reason can be given either within themselves or by some sufficiently simply hypothesis common to them; next, it is coherent if it

17

conforms to the customary nature of other phenomena which have repeatedly occurred to us, so that its parts have the same position, order,
and outcome in relation to the phenomenon which similar phenomena
have had. Otherwise phenomena will be suspect, for if we were to see
men moving through the air astride the hippogryphs of Ariostus, it
would, I believe, make us uncertain whether we were dreaming or
awake.[11]

Leibniz proceeds to elaborate this criterion in considerable detail:

But this criterion can be referred back to another general class of tests
drawn from preceding phenomena. The present phenomenon must be
coherent with these if, namely, it preserves the same consistency or if a
reason can be supplied for it from preceding phenomena or if all together are coherent with the same hypothesis, as if with a common
cause. But certainly a most valid criterion is a consensus with the whole
sequence of life, especially if many others affirm the same thing to be
coherent with their phenomena also, for it is not only probable but certain, as I will show directly, that other substances exist which are similar to us. Yet the most powerful criterion of the reality of phenomena,
sufficient even by itself, is success in predicting future phenomena from
past and present ones, whether that prediction is based upon a reason,
upon a hypothesis that was previously successful, or upon the customary consistency of things as observed previously.[12]

Thus Leibniz laid down two fundamental criteria for the distinguishing
of real from imaginary phenomena; the vividness and complexity of inner
detail on the one hand and the coherence and lawfulness of mutual rela-
tionship upon the other.

Thus Leibniz, Platonist that he self-avowedly was, followed the master's coherentist lead in this connection. Over and above the manifold of
provable truth in mathematics he envisioned a further domain of factual
rather than formal truth grounded in general principles of rational order
("systemic fitness")—a realm which encompasses the fundamental principles of natural philosophy.

C. I. LEWIS

C. I. Lewis maintains that the first principles of our knowledge emerge as such through retrospective certification by considerations of pragmatic efficacy. They are first not in a developmental sense but rather in order of fundamentality and importance with respect to the range of application at issue. And this emergence only with the wisdom of hindsight after we have seen how useful in matters of systematization and—especially—of application and implementation those principles prove to be. On this basis, the approach of C. I. Lewis to first principles was essentially one of Pragmatism.

GÖDEL

As Kurt Gödel saw it, the first principles of mathematics are certified by a conceptual (rather than sensory) mode of intuitive insight (cataleptic conrather than perception) into an absolute realms of mathematical truth and reality. And, on this basis, for Gödel, as for Leibniz before him, there is a Platonic realism of theoretical fact based not on human preferences but in inherent harmonization within the rational economy of the larger scheme of things.

And so Gödel's line of thought took the essentially Platonic line: Mathematics/arithmetic is a matter not of abstract necessity—of (axiomatic provability/demonstrability) but sometimes requires rational explicability (on grounds of fundamental principles of harmony/elegance/rational economy), thereby becoming a matter of *validation* through considerations of rational harmony rather than axiomatic *demonstration*.

In her stimulating book on Gödel, Rebecca Goldstein has it that "Gödel like so many lovers of abstraction, has found in Plato a vision of reality that amounted to intellectual love."[13] But there is simply too much spincontrol going on here. What drew Gödel to Plato was his belief not merely in the reality of the abstract but in the rationality of what is real—abstractions included. The pivot of Gödel's outlook was not intellectual love (the *amor intellectualis* of Spinoza) but rather a Leibnizian faith in the harmonious order of reality—in the paramount role of mathematical rationality in the larger scheme of things. As regards the presently contemplated taxonomies of approaches to first principles, Gödel was a coherentist of a Platonic stamp.

4. THE CONTEXTUALITY OF FIRST PRINCIPLES

The very diversity of thought that confronts us in this area itself carries an instructive lesson. As the example of Aristotle already indicates, there is no cogent reason of general principle why a recourse to first principles and their validation should be uniform: why different approaches should not appertain to the first principles of different disciplines and different subject-matter domains. Notwithstanding one's natural preference for uniform solutions, there would seem to be good reason why the case-specific complexion of different contexts of knowledge should not call for a different treatment here. For to all appearances it is only to be expected that different subject-matter domains should stand differently with regard to the way in which their first principles are secured and legitimated. The following considerations indicate the reasonable possibilities along these lines.

• *Everyday knowledge of perceptual/observations of particular fact.*

Here the plausible policy would seem to be a Processist approach, adopting the defeasibilistic line of taking our perceptual experience at face value and letting its deliverances to count as authorized knowledge until proven otherwise.

• *Everyday knowledge of common-sense factual generalizations.*

Here the sensible policy might well be a coherentist Pragmatistic approach to these so-called first principles as probatively last via provisional acceptance and "proof-of-the-pudding" style retrojustification via functional efficacy and appliative effectiveness.

• *Knowledge of scientific fact.*

Here it could seem to be sensible policy to adopt a Coherentism which sees first principles as products of systematization—that is, as acquiring the stature of firstness on the basis of their eventual standing as the systemic organization of our knowledge in a coherent expository accounting.

• *Mathematical knowledge.*

Here it seems sensible in the first instance to take a Self-Evidentistic approach and regard the initial first principles as self-evidentiating. Subsequently, further principles could then be added by way of a coherentist systematization and reconstitute one's view of firstness in the retrospective light of coherentist systematization.

As this view of the terrain indicates, it makes perfectly good sense to adapt the remedy to the malady—to let the resolution of the problem of first principles be attuned to the problem-setting circumstance of the epistemic context rather than insisting upon any universal across-the-board remedy. On such a pluristically diversified approach, no attempt would be made to contemplate a uniform treatment of first principles. Instead, the issue of the appropriate mode of firstness would be seen as context-depicted with each of the classical approaches would be deemed operable within some appropriate sphere. The validation of first principles would thus be seen inherently differentiated with respect to the specific domain of consideration.

But where would such a pluralistically case-specific approach leave philosophy—the realm in which first principles were initially brought upon the stage of consideration by Plato and Aristotle?

5. FIRST PRINCIPLES IN PHILOSOPHY

Principles of thought-procedure have played a prominent role throughout the history of philosophy.[14] But what of the issue of fundamentals here? What are the first principles of philosophizing and how do they come to be determined as such?

At the level of fundamentals, first principles can in general be classified as follows:

• *Procedural* in relation to the modus operandi of rational discourse and deliberation at large.

• *Substantive* in relation to the de facto circumstances of various specific sorts of objects of consideration.

—*Disciplinary* in relation to the select objects of special disciplines.

—*Trans-disciplinary* or *metaphysical* in relation to objects-at-large and being-in-general.

Procedural principles are by their very nature doctrinally neutral: they require no substantive commitment to the lay of the land in various domains. Like the principles of logic they relate to the conditions for merely *discussing* (rather than actually *describing*) things at the level of generality at issue with being-in-general. Moreover, the substantive principles of metaphysics will (as such) have to be trans-disciplinary addressing the nature of the reality as-a-whole, holding that things at large are fundamentally of this or that nature. Materialism, idealism, monism, dualism, pluralism, all these are matters of *describing* reality, and all go well beyond the basics that enable us to operate effectively in rational inquiring and deliberation.

On this basis these distinctions we shall have to distinguish between the

- first principles of *philosophizing* (i.e., the basic procedure ground-rules for cultivating philosophy).

and

- first principles in *philosophy* (regarding this or the other sort of a doctrinal position in the field).

A first principle of philosophizing should be seen as a general instruction for cogent deliberation, a maxim that lays down a methodological rule for philosophical practice. This will involve such contentions as: "Never characterize something as a (concrete) identifiable thing if you are not prepared to claim that it admits of identification, and also classification, and beyond this even of description." This sort of principle is not a philosophical thesis or doctrine that purports to answer to some substantive philosophical question. Instead, it is a rule of procedure that specifies a modus operandi, a way of proceeding in the course of philosophizing. Such a methodological principle is to philosophy what a maxim like "always keep your promises" is to morality. It represents a guideline to be followed if effective praxis in the field is to be realized. Such methodological principles are general rules of procedure, framed in terms of maxims that prescribe the appropriateness or inappropriateness of different ways of proceeding in philosophizing.[15]

By contrast, it transpires that *within* philosophy one also encounters a profusion of principles of a natural or substantive nature. In ethics there is the "Principle of Utility" holding that the rightness of an action lies in its capacity to conduce to the greatest good of the greatest number, in natural philosophy we have the "Principle of Causality" holding that every event has a cause, or in epistemology the "Principle of Truth" that only what is true can be said to be known to someone: $(\exists x)Kxp \rightarrow p$. Such principles are principles IN philosophy not principles OF philosophizing, that is, are not procedural principles of philosophizing.[16]

But can process and product be separated in this domain? Must reality itself not cooperate in this enterprise in being such that these concepts apply to it in some ontologically fundamental way?

The fact of it is that there is indeed something ontological which argues for such procedural principles, namely the factor of functional efficacy. After all, philosophizing is a purposive enterprise. It has an aim or mission— to enable us to orient ourselves in thought and action, enabling us to get a clearer understanding of the big issues of our place and our prospects in a complex world that is not of our own making. And the validation of those procedural principles that are philosophically first must in the final analysis rest on its promise and performance in fostering this enterprise.

As Aristotle already insisted, the principle of Contradiction—to the effect that one should never accept logically incompatible theses—clearly illustrates the pragmatic basis of philosophical first principles. After all, the endorsement of truths and the rejection of falsehoods as one of the prime objectives of the entire venture of rational inquiry. And in asserting mutually contradictory theses we at once ensure that our body of accepted information will include falsehoods. And more generally, we do well to accept that reality conforms to the fundamental principles of logic, not because this is somehow predetermined as a basic ontological fact (though in some manner it undoubtedly is), but because without making this supposition from the outset we doom the enterprise of rational inquiry to impotent failure.

Such a two-sided approach to philosophical first principles turns on the distinction between *theses* and *methods*, propositions and procedures. For it proposed to see the first principles of philosophy not as substantive contentions (philosophical theses or doctrines) but rather as procedural methods: they are not constitutive and substantive but rather regulative and procedure (to use Kant's terminology). And first principles of philosophy would on this basis not be substantiated by inferential argumentation of

some sort—let alone by insight or induction. Instead they would be validated pragmatically through the consideration of this utility and efficacy on
the particular domain at practice that is at issue.

There is, perhaps, something a bit ironic about this. For it means that in
the end the fundamentals of our philosophizing—the most theoretical enterprise of all—are to be essential and legitimated by the essentially practi-
calistic standard of purposive efficacy (though, to be sure, the purposes at
issue will themselves relate to matter of theorizing). To the content of the
pragmatists, it transpires that even here, in this most theoretical of domains, the issues of function and purpose cannot be left aside.

NOTES FOR CHAPTER 2

[1] See Aristotle, *Metaphysics* Δ1, 1013a16-18. Pre-eminently something akin to Aristotle's prime mover will be at issue here.

[2] Plato, *The Republic*, VII, 533-34.

[3] Plato, *Timaeus*, 48A.

[4] On the relevant issues see James Lennox, "Aristotle's Problems," *Ancient Philosophy*, vol. 14 (1994), pp. 53-77.

[5] Compare T. H. Irwin, *Aristotle's First Principles* (Oxford: Clarendon Press, 1988).

[6] On the relevant issues see Alan Code, "Aristotle's Investigation of a Basic Logical
Principle," *Canadian Journal of Philosophy*, vol. 16 (1986), pp. 341-58.

[7] On the medieval context at large see the excellent discussion in John Longeway's
article on "Medieval Theories of Demonstration" in the *Stanford Encyclopedia of
Philosophy*.

[8] Sententia super *Posteriora analytica*, I, 4.

[9] This sort of thing is a vivid percussion of Edmund Husserl's *Wesensschau*.

[10] Gerhardt, *Phil.* VII, pp. 319-20; Loemker, pp. 363-4.

[11] *Phil.*, VII, p. 329; Loemker, p. 364.

[12] *Ibid.*

NOTES FOR CHAPTER 2

[13] Goldstein, p. 260.

[14] For more details see the author's essay "Principia Philosophiae" in *The Review of Metaphysics*, vol. 56 (2006), pp. 3-17.

[15] Recall that to be a "man of principles" is to honor the rules, to "play it by the book" and not to see oneself entitled to count as an exception—entitled to have things one's own way irrespective of the rules that hold for others.

[16] Logic is something of an exception here since it is (traditionally seen as) a part of philosophy as well as a guide to its conduct. Because the principles of logic represent requisites of cogent communication in general, they hold ubiquitously in all domains—and accordingly govern sensible philosophical discourse as well.

Chapter 3

THE HUME-EDWARDS PRINCIPLE AND ITS PROBLEMS

1. THE HUME-EDWARDS PRINCIPLE

In formulating a version of the Cosmological Argument for the existence of God, Samuel Clarke and Leibniz shared the conviction that accounting for existence of the universe-as-a-whole requires explanatory resort to something above and beyond the universe itself.[1] Reacting against this line of thought David Hume wrote:

> Did I show you the particular cause of each individual in a collection of twenty particles of matter, I should think that it very unreasonable, should you afterwards ask me, what was the cause of the whole twenty. This is sufficiently explained in explaining the cause of the parts.[2]

The underlying idea is far older, however. Thus William of Ockham wrote in ca. 1320:

> The whole multitude of ... causes is indeed caused, but neither by any one thing that is part of this multitude nor by something outside this multitude, but rather one part is caused by one thing which is part of this multitude, and another by another thing, and so on ad infinitum.[3]

And later traces of this line of thinking can be found in many critics of the Cosmological Argument from Immanuel Kant[4] down to such 20th century writers as Paul Edwards.[5] And so in reviewing the literature of the problem, William R. Rowe dubbed the underlying idea at issue the "Hume-Edwards Principle", formulating it as follows:

> If the existence of every member of a set is explained the existence of that set is thereby explained.[6]

In unison with this line of thought, philosophers of positivist inclinations often maintain that we should reject all general explanations for reality-at-large and pursue our efforts at understanding the world in a disaggregated, piece-meal manner. They insist that in matters of ontology we should not try to account for existence-at-large in one all-encompassing collective explanation, but simply try to account for the reality's several constituent elements in a way that proceeds in a disaggregated, seriatim manner. And in line with this perspective they tend to eschew the global and synoptic perspective of the accustomed "big questions" of the philosophical tradition.

The thinkers of this tendency (Hume and Edwards themselves included) have seen the Hume-Edwards Principle as an instrument of ontological simplification (or indeed even purification) and have viewed its salient lesson as lying in the implicit injunction: "Don't trouble to ask for a *collective* explanation of existence-at-large, a comprehensive *distributive* explanation of the particular existents will provide you everything you need and want." Yet notwithstanding its widespread acceptance and influential impact, the principle is deeply problematic—not to say wrong.

2. COUNTEREXAMPLES

It is not hard to find prima facie counter-examples to the Hume-Edwards thesis:

- If the existence of each book in its collection is explained the existence of the library-as-a-whole is thereby explained.

- If the existence of each part of the car is explained, the existence of the vehicle-as-a-whole is thereby explained.

- If the existence of each composition in our symphony's evening program is explained, the existence of the program-as-a-whole is thereby explained.

Such examples cast a deep shadow of doubt over the Hume-Edwards thesis. For it is only too obvious that to explain and account for the existence of the words does little to explain or account for the existence of the sentence. To do the latter we would have to account not merely for the existence of those words but for their collective co-presence *in that particular context*. Component oriented existence explanations that do not account for contextual co-presence within a pre-specified entirety cannot explain its existence. Explaining the parts may achieve nothing whatever towards explaining the existence of wholes. For wholes must, as such, have a unifying identity and thus an explanation of their constituents viewed separately and individually does not suffice to provide it. Nor does explaining each event in a series explain its entire course, much as understanding each sentence may fail to explain understanding the whole book.

In other words, the Hume-Edwards thesis suffers from a critical flaw of omission. For where the parts of wholes are concerned, *context makes for structure*. It does not suffice to note that we are dealing with a three letter word in which the letters *D*, *G*, and *O* figure co-presently, seeing that there yet remains the massive difference between *GOD* and *DOG*.

Moreover, the aspect of explanation and understanding can be put aside and the principle viewed ontologically rather than epistemically to in the form:

If every part of a whole exists, then so does the whole itself.

or

If every member of a collectivity exists, then so does that collectivity itself.

The preceding examples of libraries, automobiles, and symphony programs shows that this transformed version of the Hume-Edwards Principle also does not work. Only within totally unstructured collectivities (such as the mathematicians' set) will the envisioned relationships obtain. So if—contrary to fact—our sole concern were with the abstract rudimentary "sets" of the set theory (*Mengenlehre*) of pure mathematics, the problem would not arise. Those mathematical "sets" are defined purely extensionally on the basis of their membership alone: they have no form or structure whatsoever. But this circumstance is realized only in abstractions and never concretely. And in any other setting—even that of the "*ordered* sets" of pure mathematics—what the principle claims just is not so. In general, the world's wholes always have a characteristic structure and could not be what they are without it.

The inherent problem of the Hume-Edwards Principle accordingly comes to the fore when one steps back to consider just what it would take to fix it. And this comes to light in considering a reformulation of the thesis by the addition of a few crucial and critical words.

> If the existence of each part of a whole is explained *in conjunction with an account that also explains their mutual coordination within the larger overarching setting of that whole*, then the existence of that whole is thereby explained.

As this amplification shows, that which is missing from the Hume-Edwards thesis—and engenders the flaw from which all of those counter-examples—is the lack of an account of the co-existence of those several constituents *as parts of the whole in question*. For only an explanation of the existence of the parts of a whole is their role as constituting parts of that specific whole will explain the existence of that whole.

It is this holistic demand—a factor which most exponents of the Hume-Edwards Principle deem anathema—that is indispensably required for the viability of the principle.[7]

The long and short of it is that the Hume-Edwards thesis radically over-simplifies the actual situation. For it rides roughshod over the consideration that over and above items or objects there are structures (patterns, forms of order) that can organize those items into different sorts of wholes, and that throughout our concerns with collectivities these structures matter. And it does not matter whether the structure is processual/temporal rather than physical/geometric. (To explain the existence of each issue of a complex menu does not account for the meal-as-a-whole.) The Hume-Edwards Principle radically oversimplifies the actual situation by failing to reckon with the holistic aspect of the situation. To explain the parts severally and distributively simply does not account for the collective unity at issue with their coordinate co-existence as part of one single whole. The inherent logic of the situation is such that in asking for a collective explanation of existence one is stating a demand that no merely distributive explanation—however extensive and elaborate—is able to meet.

3. VARIANT VERSIONS OF PAN-EXPLICABILITY

The Hume-Edwards Principle fails to heed certain critical *conceptual* distinctions that are readily brought to light by means of a bit of symbolic machinery. So let us adopt the following abbreviations:

$p @ q$ for "*p* [is true and] provides an adequate explanatory account for *q*", where the variables *p* and *q* range over factual claims.

E!x for "*x* exists", where the variable *x* ranges over existing objects.

Since the variable *x* ranges over existents, we have it that $(\forall x)E!x$.

On this basis it is readily brought to view that the form of the statement "Everything has an explanation" or "There is an explanation for everything" admits of two very different constructions:

Distributive explanation: "There is some case-specific explanation to account for each and any existential fact."

(1) $(\forall x)(\exists p)(p @ E!x)$

Collective explanation: "There is one single generic explanation that accounts for all existential facts—each and every one of them."

(2) $(\exists p)(\forall x)(p @ E!x)^8$

As these specifications indicate, two decidedly different questions can be at issue, namely:

• Does every existent have its own (individual) existence-explanation?

• Is the one self-same single explanation that suffices to account for the existence of each of the things that exists?

To be sure, we have it that $(2) \rightarrow (1)$, but of course the converse does not hold. The Hume-Edwards thesis proceeds on the mistaken idea that it does. Different questions are at issue and different matters are at stake with distinctive and collective explanations. And in posing different questions we must be prepared for the possibility of different answers.

4. SOME CONTEMPLATED ACCOMMODATION

Why is it that those considerations about the role of structure actually tell against the Hume-Edwards Principle?

In most cases, objects are like children's play-blocks—items that can be assembled in various ways and their own existence thereby nowise explains the existence of the whole of which they can be components. The same components, in sum, can in principle conjoin differently to make up different wholes. But it would seem on first thought that the universe-as-a-whole is going to be an exception here. After all there is—and (ex hypothesis) only can be—just one of these, so that irrespective of how the components get assembled there will be only one single all-embracing totality. The idea of there actually being different universes is highly problematic.[9] And in consequence the issue of structure becomes irrelevant and the preceding objections to the Hume-Edwards thesis fall aside.

On this basis the Hume-Edwards aficionados might argue as follows in endeavoring to meet the thrust of the preceding strictures:

> In resorting to the Hume-Edwards Principle we have one very special application in mind. For our aim is to dismiss the request for one single comprehensive explanation of existence-at-large. And it is here that we want to insist on the need for distributive rather than collective explanation. Our concern is not with such micro-collectivities as words or books or cars or symphony programs. Our concern is with Reality-as-a-whole. The trouble with all those proposed counter-examples—books in a collection, part of an automobile, musical pieces in a program—is that in each case those items could be assembled otherwise than as-is, and could in principle belong to different wholes. But this is not so with the physical constitution of the actual universe—the totality of existents. All of those counter-examples rest on a misleading analogy. The world's constituents cannot be differently assembled into different universes. There is and can be only one universe. To think of it as possibly different is to ignore the inherent necessity of things. Once we have (and have explained) the existence of these constituents there is nothing left to explain.

However, this defense will not do. For even if it is acknowledged that there is, in principle, only one single all-embracing universe, this Principle of Universe Uniqueness will actually leave the real issue untouched. The reality of it is that even if we abandon the idea of *different* (*possible*) *universes*, we still have at our beck and call the idea of *different possibilities for* the constituents of this *universe*—the one and only actual one. And this factor of different possibilities suffices to keep the structure-oriented objection in play. For the requisite uniqueness could be achieved only by reducing to one not just the number of universes, but even the number of possibilities for a universe. Only at the price of commitment to a block-universe of the necessitarian dismissal of alternative possibilities could the Hume-Edwards Principle be maintained in the face of structural considerations.

5. A LAST-DITCH STAND

In endeavoring something of a last-ditch stand, Hume-Edwards partisans might take a very different line as follows:

You misunderstand us. We are actually not trying to enunciate an explanatory *principle* at all. Rather, our concern is with a procedural *policy*; we want to urge a certain line of approach to the global explanation of existence. Our position is not that of the stricture: "Don't bother to ask for a collective explanation of existence at large because a distributive explanation will give you everything you want." Our position is, rather, "Don't go so far as to ask for a collective explanation for existence at large because this is asking for too much. For global explanation is something inherently unrealizable. A distributive explanation of existence is the best and the most that one can ever hope to get."

However, to endorse this policy-recommendation is—clearly!—something quite different from accepting the Hume-Edwards Principle as a factual thesis, and any victory that could be gained by this particular defense is Pyrrhic. For in taking this line one does not support—or even invoke—the Hume-Edwards thesis as generally understood, but actually abandons it. Moreover, once the idea is abandoned that the policy rests on a correct and cogent principle, then *justifying* that policy emerges to saddle its exponent with a heavy burden of proof—one that goes counter to much of the philosophic tradition and requires its exponents to embark on a large and deeply problematic project.

What does all of this mean for the Cosmological Argument? It serves to indicate that Leibniz and Clarke were right at least in this, that explaining the existence of the universe-as-a-whole is something that encompasses a distinctive demand over and above a putative explanation of existence of the individual components involved. That mega-issue is not to be sidelined by a disintegrative principle of the sort envisioned by Hume and Edwards.

In the final analysis their thesis fails in its aspiration to provide a little instrument for sidelining a big issue.

NOTES FOR CHAPTER 3

[1]   See Samuel Clarke, *A Demonstration of the Being and Attribute of God* (London, 1705), and G. W. Leibniz, *Monadology*, sect.s 37-38.

[2]   David Hume, *Dialogues Concerning Natural Religion* (Edinburgh: 1779), Part IX. See also Joseph K. Campbell, "Hume's Refutation of the Cosmological Argument," *International Journal for the Philosophy of Religion*, vol. 40 (1996), pp. 159-73.

[3]   William of Ockham, *Philosophical Writings*, ed. by P. Boehner (Edinburg: Nelson, 1957), p. 124.

[4]   A deep distrust of aggregative totalization pervades the whole first section of "The Antinomy of Pure Reason" in the *Critique of Pure Reason*.

[5]   Paul Edwards, "The Cosmological Argument," *The Rationalist Annual for the Year 1959* (London: Pemberton, 1960 [??]), reprinted in Donald R. Burrell (ed.), *The Cosmological Argument* (New York: Doubleday, 1967).

[6]   William R. Rowe, "Two Criticism of the Cosmological Argument," *The Monist*, vol. 54 (1970); reprinted in W. L. Rowe and W. Wainwright (eds.) *Philosophy of Religion: Selective Readings*, 2nd edition (New York: Harcourt Brace Jovanavich, 1989), pp. 142-56. (See p. 153.) On this principle see also Richard M. Gale, *On the Nature and Existence of God* (Cambridge: Cambridge University Press, 1991), and Alexander R. Pruss, "The Hume-Edwards Principle and the Cosmological Argument," *International Journal for Philosophy of Religion*, vol. 434 (1988), pp. 149-65.

[7]   Note that the cognate thesis "If every member of a collection has a certain property then so does the collection as a whole" is obviously in trouble. It works just fine with arguments like "If every part of a machine is made of iron, then the machine-as-a-whole is made of iron." Or "If every part of a field is in Pennsylvania then so is the field as a whole." But it fails grievously to obtain in general, seeing that it commits the so-called Fallacy of Composition. Every member of the collection may well fit in this box without this being true of the entire collection. Or consider a mathematical example. Every member of the series {1}, {1,2}, {1, 2 3} etc. is a finite set, but the series-as-a-whole certainly is not. As Patterson Brown has rightly observed, with inference by composition "each such proof must be considered on its own merits". See his "Infinite Causal Regression" in Anthony Kenny (ed.),

NOTES FOR CHAPTER 3

Aquinas: A Collection of Critical Essays (Notre Dame: University of Notre Dame Press, 1976), pp. 214-236. (See p. 230.)

[8] Note that neither of these is the same as $(\exists p)(p\ @\ (\forall x)E!x)$ which obtains trivially given the symbolic conventions adopted here.

[9] Actually this is an exaggeration in the face of multiverse theory in quantum cosmology. Here the issue has to be kicked upstairs, subject to the idea that it is the multiverse rather than the universe that is of necessity unique.

Chapter 4

THE LIMITS OF NATURALISM (NATURE AND CULTURE IN PERSPECTIVAL DUALITY)

1. TWO MODES OF "NATURALISM"

Naturalism has two principal senses. In the one it is simply a euphemism for scientism as such—the idea being that science has all the answers—that if there is going to be any answer to a question about reality, it will be forthcoming from natural science. Its stance is that of a science-know-all reductionism and it sees the key to understanding reality provided for by the instrumentalities that account for the fundamental processes of the observable phenomena. The other—nowadays far less usual sense of the term—envisions nature as a humanly user-friendly setting that has provided for the emergence of intelligent beings capable of understanding and explaining—to at least *some* extent—how nature works. The crux of this *idealistic* (rather than *scientistic*) version of naturalism lies not in the idea of *reduction* of intelligence and its works to the material realities of nature, but rather in seeing the latter as so constituted as to produce an environment congenial to the emergence of intelligent beings. In consequence there is both a positivistic or scientistic and a humanistic construal of naturalism—typified by neo-Darwinism on the one hand and the emergent evolutionism of Bergson on the other. Both versions envision the fundamentality of natural process—one focusing on the *development* of life in nature, the other on the functioning of *intelligence* in nature.

2. A DUAL REALITY

In line with this duality of approach, the ontological perspective of Western philosophical thought has from its very outset been dualistic. From the days of Presocratics it has distinguished the realm of *phusis* (nature) and of *nomos* (artifice)—of physical reality on the one hand, and on the other human contrivance such as language or custom. And various

Greek thinkers already transmuted this distinction into one between two existential levels—the one deep, fundamental, and natural, the other shallow, derivative, and artificial; the former geared to realty, the latter to mere appearance.[1] Plato picked up these threads of thought and transformed them into a distinction between the sensory world—the world of the everyday life observation—and an ideal world accessible to reason alone. As he saw it, it is the mind rather than the senses that provides the proper pathway to reality. And Judeo-Christian thought reinforced this dualization, taking the line that after the expulsion from Eden man was constrained to have his life in this imperfect world, albeit ever conscious of (and yearning for) an ideal world inaccessible to mundane experience. Neo-Platonism and the Church fathers followed along the tracks of this tradition.

And so, the perspectival duality of nature and nurture, the physical and the conceptual realm has been among the most fundamental and pervasive features of Western philosophy. Its dialectic of philosophical deliberations moved within the range defined by the two poles of mind and matter, with mankind generally seen as an amphibian able to live in two distinct realms.

With Leibniz this dualization took the form of two distinct orders—the kingdoms of nature and of grace—the former entirely mechanical, the later entirely teleological, and the two coordinated by a pre-established harmony between matters and spirit. Immanuel Kant moved this dualization forward. For him too, man is an amphibian living in two distinct realms, the experiential world of nature ruled by natural law and efficient causation and a nominal world of intelligence, rationality, and free will governed by the agent-causality of rational beings. On the one hand scientifically inquiring reason can and should proceed to explain everything in scientific principles; but on the other side a different order with its own teleological principles is free to explain human activities in very different terms of reference. Two distinct explanatory worlds are thus at issue: the realm of natural causality (causality of nature) and that of nomic causality (causality of thought). With the duality of our living at once in the realm of nature and also that of the thought-artifice characteristic of homo sapiens.

3. AN AMBIDEXTROUS TRADITION

While German idealism rebelled against Kant on through its impersonalistic naturalization of "Spirit", its post-Hegelian successors—specifically Friedrich Rickert, Johann Eduard Erdmann, and Wilhelm Dilthey—

returned once more to a Kant-reminiscent dualistic perspective, with the idea of man's occupancy of a dual world again coming to the fore. Thus Dilthey envisioned a naturalistic world-oriented empirical science and a humanistic and normatively oriented study for the human condition. On the one side lay the natural world (*Naturwelt*) of the natural and exact sciences (*Naturwissenschaften*); on the other the world of everyday life (*Lebenswelt*: life-world). The latter is predicated on the artifacts of culture and society whose lineaments inhere in the thought-framework afforded us by processes that we study in the human rather than natural sciences (the *Geisteswissenschaften* rather than the *Naturwissenschaften*). And these thinkers saw it, the two domains of nature and culture do not—cannot—really conflict, both because they deal with different matters (physical processes and conceptual processes) and because they must in the final analysis be comparable given that human thought transpires within the format of nature.

And so two distinct modes of reality were deemed to be at issue throughout this tradition, recurring again and again in the repeated Leitmotif. The 20th century affords ample illustrations of this. C. P. Snow's two intellectual cultures have often figured in the thought and discourse of academic inquirers. Think here of Sir Arthur Eddington's two tables. Wilfred Sellars' distinction between the "scientific image" of things and the "manifest image" by which we deal with them in everyday life. Or, again, that of John McDowell's distinction between the scientific-explanatory space of causes and the anthropocentric-conceptualistic space of reasons—as well as the present author's distinction between the natural order of causality and the thought-order of ideals. All of these are, at bottom, simply so many later-day variations on the theme of Dilthey's fundamental duality.

What has become particularly prominent in the 20th century is a dualism of fact and value, of observational information about the world and affective judgments from a humane perspective.

And this line of thinking confronts us with a duality of realms: natural science and humanistic culture. Science uses causal explanation to embark the life-world within the natural order; humanism uses hermeneutic explanation to fit science into the life-world as a human project. The scientific order is causally reductive; the humane order is hermeneutically constructive.

4. A PRAGMATIC LINKAGE

Which of these two competing perspectives upon reality at large, the humanistic and the scientistic, is the correct one—or at least which is the more fundamental? The answer in the final analysis is: neither one. Like waking and sleeping both are coordinatively necessary to achieve a healthy balance in the understanding of reality.

After all, how are the two worlds—the observational scientific natural-world and the experiential life-world—related to one another? The question is fundamental, and the answer is simple. The glue that links the two together is explanation. But different modes of *explanation* are at issue: the one, causal explanation, proceeds in the natural scientists' domain of matter and energy and the other, hermeneutical explanation, proceeds within the reference frame of a humanistic sphere of purpose and value. And the situation that results overall is one of coordinative unity engendered by the realities of man's place within nature.

One can, of course, choose to be one-sided about it. If you want to be a reductive scientific materialist you opt for the perspective of natural science. If you want to be a cultural idealist you opt for the perspective of imaginative humanism. However, if you want to be a synoptic realist you will do well to take both into stride at once as per the bi-polar synthesis Figure 1. You will then accept a complex reality that envisions a two-sided intertwining of the two, effectively adopt a complex-reality perspective that combines and coordinates causal naturalism with hermeneutic idealism.

Man indeed is an amphibious creature, destined to live in the realm of physical materiality and mental conceptuality. And given that we actually can "have it both ways" there is no good reason why we should not.

And so what we do well to accept in the end is a systemically integrated perspective that comes to terms with two fundamental facts (1) that homo sapiens exists and has his being within the world of nature as science studies it, and (2) that science itself is a human construction whose ideas, concepts, and theories are cultural artifacts of the conceptual order.

Figure 1

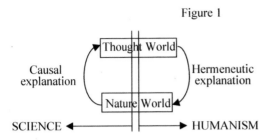

A theory of nature that cannot be articulated via artifice-devised conceptualizations. A manifold of concepts that cannot come to grips with natural reality through application and prediction is blind. To achieve cognitive health, the two sectors must collaborate and interact in fruitful symbiosis to facilitate a Janus-forced duality of perspective that look alike to the workings of nature and of mind.

5. THE FUTURE OF NATURALISM

What links natural reality and its cognitive artifice together is the factor of *application*—the fact that we use the conceptual construction of our science to guide our action within nature in ways over which we have no control, because what happens when we act—the actual results of our thought-grounded actions—is something over which we have no control. And if this recognition of application as providing conjointly a monitor of theory and an article of culture is pragmatism, then we do well to make the most of it.[2]

What then of the future of naturalism?

How naturalism will fare will very much depend on how the position is to be construed. At the outset we contemplated one mode of one-sidedness reductive scientism. Our subsequent deliberations have opened the door to yet another sort of one-sidedness that looks to what is a characteristic part of *human* nature, namely the free-wheeling speculation that beguiles our species in its more imaginatively creative moments. The outlook for both of these perspectives is bleak, simply because they are too one-sidedly narrow in outlook and perspective to come to satisfactory terms with a complex realty. The only sort of naturalism that can lay claim to a promising future will have to be one that is sufficiently broad in its range and its sympathies to allow both the nature-geared sciences (the *Naturwissen-schaften*, broadly construed), and the thought-geared insights of the humanistic sphere of ideation (the *Geisteswissenschaften*, broadly construed), to play a key role. In the end, then, it is an idealistic rather than scientistic sort of naturalism that meets the needs of coming to grips with the complex reality that confronts us. And so, it seems to me that the sort of naturalism that has a promising future will be one that is sufficiently ample in scope to do full justice both to the works of nature itself and to those of man operating within its realm.

NOTES FOR CHAPTER 4

[1] Think here not only of the Atomists but also of Heracleitus and Pythagoras.

[2] This chapter formed the core of a paper of the same title to be presented at a conference on "The Future of Naturalism" at the University of Buffalo in September 2007.

Chapter 5

ON UNIVERSALS, NATURAL KINDS, AND LAWS OF NATURE

1. QUESTIONS REGARDING UNIVERSALS

The principal questions regarding universals are six:

1. What are they?

2. In what manner (if any) can they be said to be, to exist?

3. What is their ontological dependency status, in the sense of the question: "If there were no *X*s, there would be no universals?"

4. Do they have a common nature or character?

5. Do they have a history; do or can they originate in time?

6. What is their function; what work do they do for us?

The present discussion will in due course address each of these.

2. WHAT ARE UNIVERSALS AND IN WHAT MANNER DO THEY EXIST?

The issue of what universals are pivots their contrast with concrete objects. Concreta exist in space, but universals have a generality that precludes their actual being in space. To be sure, they can indeed be repeatedly *instantiated* in spatio-temporal concreta, seeing that they are abstract in a way that admits of their realization and replication in concrete things as facets, features, or functions thereof, without themselves admitting of spatial placement. But they cannot themselves be concretely realized there. Shapes, colors, and numbers—qualities and quantities in short—afford paradigm examples of such repeatedly-instantiables.

Lacking concrete reality, then, universals do not exist themselves in spatio-material form. Only concrete particulars will admit of this. Their being such as it is, falls outside the manifold of concretely spatial existence; insofar as they exist they exist on another plane of being, one nearer to possibility than to reality as such. For universes *to be* is *to be possibly instantiated*. This potential repetitiveness characterizes universals as such.

Does the failure of universals as such to form part of concrete existence make universals into creatures of the mind?

In his *Commentary on the Isagoge of Porphyry*, Boethius asked with regard to universals "whether they exit [in themselves] or whether they have a place merely in the intellect alone; whether they are corporeal or incorporeal; and whether they have a place separate from sensibles or exist dependently upon them."[1] And so the pivotal question arises: are universals creatures of thought that exist in the intellect alone (so that their being lies in being thought), or do they actually exist in their own right—outside the domain of mind? The crucial question, in effect, is whether universals would vanish from the scene if there were no intelligences, or whether they possess a mode of being independently of the machinations of mind. It is—or should be—clear that they will not do so.

3. THE MEDIEVALS

What then are universals? The schoolmen of the Middle Ages envisioned three different lines of response here, and different schools of thought developed which held, respectively, that universals are—

- *Thought-things* existing as ideas in the mind alone (*in mente*)—as mere thought-devices for deliberation about things. So no minds, no universals. (Nominalism)

- *Features or facets of concreta* which exist in thought coherence human minds can come to cognize them by abstraction. They exist *in the concrete things themselves* (*in res*) whence they are able to be accessed by minds as thing-shared features cognized through abstractions. So, no individual particulars, no universals. (Conceptualism)

- *Supra-natural or extra-natural factors that themselves* somehow exist in reality outside nature and apart from its multitude of things and minds—though capable of instantiation and exemplified in nature's concreta. They exist *in and of themselves*, even in (potential) separation form concrete things (*ante res*). Universals exist in their own right—things or no things. (Realism)

According to these three medieval theories, then, universals exist in the mind, in things, and in (and of) themselves, respectively. They are, correspondingly, to be seen as mind-creatures, as thing-features, or as transcendentals. This being how the Schoolmen viewed the matter, the question nevertheless remains: are these indeed the only options?

4. THE DIVERSITY OF UNIVERSALS

The problem with the medieval theory, elegant though it sounds, is that it is oversimple. It does not do full justice to the complexity of the phenomena. To see this clearly, it is instructive for us to consider a spectrum of the specific instances of things that can plausibly qualify as universals. After all, the kinds of universals include (among other things)—

- shapes and structures

- colors and phenomenal sense qualities

- quantities/numbers/measures

- natural kinds (as represented by thing nouns & mass nouns)

- artificial kinds

- linguistic/symbolic kinds

- plays, novels, stories, plots

- processes (structurally considered), be they natural or artefactual

- laws of nature

- rules and conventions

All of these are universals—abstracta rather than spatial concreta. And as such we can ask of them, exactly in the spirit of those medieval themes, just what is it that they depend on? What X is it that makes it true to say: If it were not for Xs then this particular sort of universal would vanish from the ontological scene.

5. QUESTIONS OF DEPENDENCY

With regard to just this issue of ontological dependency, the medievals offered us only three options: *minds, mundane things*, and *nothing whatsoever*. But the reality of it is more complex. For when we contemplate the range of available (or conceivable) productive potencies, we arrive straightaway at what looks to be a more diversified situation. For when proceeding along this line of thought we come to be faced with the following scale of conceivable agents or agencies

- The supra-natural (The ultimate root of reality: God, the Transcendent, "The force") [R]

- The Universe/Nature/The realm of concreta [U]

- Intelligent (Rational) Agents [I]

- Humans [H]

- Societies (of humans) [S]

This "ladder" is intended to reflect an order of *ontological dependency*. The idea is that if a given agency did not exist, neither would anything ranked beneath it in the scale, so that there is always a dependency status— dependence upon what is above, independence of what is below. Some things are self-subsistent and depend on nothing, some on the universe, some on intelligent beings, and so on.

On this basis, what would seem to qualify as the standard at-first-sight view of universals we arrive at the picture of Display 1.

Note that this presents a situation that envisions five possibilities rather than the mere three G, U, I contemplated by the medievals. With this extension of the range of possibilities the "problem of universals" becomes more complex than the medievals contemplated. They clearly oversimplified matters.

6. A POLYMORPHIC ONTOLOGY OF UNIVERSALS

And the medieval approach committed yet another sort of oversimplification. For the scholastic approach to the matter was based on the attempt to uniformize the status of universals. The range of alternatives that were envisioned confined itself to a uniformitarianism that had the following structure:

> NOMINALISM: All universals depend on human conventions. Universals are uniformity of type $\mathbb{S}$—or at best $\mathbb{I}$. Linguistic/symbolic kinds are paradigmatic. (Shapes and quantities now become decidedly problematic, as do natural kinds.)

> REALISM: All universals have a supra-natural status: there is no dependence on nature's concreta. Universals are uniformly of type $\mathbb{R}$. Quantities/numbers are paradigmatic. (Symbolic kinds—say letter of the alphabet—now become problematic.)[2]

> CONCEPTUALISM: All universals depend on the modus operandi of finite beings. Universals are uniformity of type $\mathbb{I}$ (or possibly $\mathbb{H}$). Letters of the alphabet are now paradigmatic. (Shapes now become problematic, as do natural kinds.)

As this survey indicates, those traditional medieval theories were committed to the uniformitarian idea that *all universals are of the same kind in point of ontological status*. And this is surely quite incorrect. For uniformity here engenders real problems since no matter which alternative one fixes on, there will be exceptions.

Display 1

THE STANDARD/NAÏVE VIEW OF UNIVERSALS

THERE WOULD BE NO	IF THERE WERE NO
—shapes and structures	$\mathbb{R}$ [or $\mathbb{U}$]
—colors and phenomenal sense quantities	$\mathbb{H}$
—quantities/numbers/measurement	$\mathbb{G}$
—natural kinds	$\mathbb{U}$
—artificial kinds	$\mathbb{I}$
—linguistic/symbolic kinds	$\mathbb{S}$
—plays, novels, stories, plots, jokes	$\mathbb{I}$
—natural processes	$\mathbb{U}$
—laws of nature	$\mathbb{R}$ [or $\mathbb{U}$]
—rules and conventions	$\mathbb{S}$

7. THE ISSUE OF TEMPORAL ORIGINATION

The big difficulty with nominalism is in relation to laws of nature; it is not easy to persuade oneself that natural thing-kinds such as water did not preexist thinking. On the other hand, the main difficulty with realism is that it is difficult to persuade oneself that sense-qualities like colors and odors have an existence apart from the world's physical things. As these considerations suggest, it is, clearly, the best plan to move beyond the medieval trichotomy to the fuller picture of five distinct—and potentially concurrent possibilities—an approach based on adopting a pluralistic theory of universals. The diversity encountered among the phenomena at issue is best and most naturally accommodated by employing a polymorphic approach to universals which acknowledges that the decidedly different sorts of things at issue require different treatment at the level of theory. Only by adopting a polymorphic rather than uniformitarian approach we can avert the obvious problems inhering in a one-size-fits-all theory of universals.

This line of thought also makes it possible to address satisfactorily some of the difficulties that caused perplexity in earlier stages of discussion.

Do universals originate in time or are they extra- or non-temporal? Are they found or are they made?

A polymorphic theory of universals can and will take a differentiated line with on these questions. Clearly shapes and quantities and other mind-independent universals will have no history. They are "eternal objects". But letters of the Roman or Greek alphabet will have a history—an origination in time. And the same can be said for those universals, which, like phenomenal colors, come into being in the course of biological history. Different sorts of universals must be viewed differently in their relation to time because they relate to human seeing and thereby cannot preexist humans.

8. THE FUNCTION OF UNIVERSALS

What work do universals do for us? For what task are they indispensably required as a conceptual resource? The answer is straightforward. We need universals—and different types of them—to deal adequately with *laws of nature* as we understand them.

A "law of nature" is exhibited paradigmatically in such simple generalizations as "Acids turn blue litmus paper red" or "Elm trees are deciduous in shedding their leaves annually in the autumn". And all such laws conform to one selfsame generic format:

Whenever conditions of type 1 are realized conditions of type 2 will occur.

But just what is the nature and status of those conditions of a particular type? The answer is again straightforward. Insofar as authentic natural laws are at issue all of those type-congeners will and must come together to form a particular natural kind. In sum, we require natural kinds in order to characterize structural coordinations that represent the idea of laws of nature as this functions within the conceptual scheme that we employ in these matters. Universals, in sum, stand coordinate with *natural kinds* in the nomologically laden sense of that term.

9. THE RATIONALE OF UNIVERSALS

What universals there are is one thing and what universals are another. And while the former issue calls for differentiation, the latter demands a unified treatment. The question "What is at bottom that makes for universals?" must be answered in a homogeneous way.

Co-instantiations is a matter of feature-sameness: All instantiations of a given universal answer to the same generic feature (shape, color, kind, etc.) as defined by that universal. Accordingly, the most fundamental fact regarding universals is what may be called the Pythagorean Thesis that universality is always a matter of structure-sameness in the sense that: All of those modes of feature-sameness can ultimately be accounted for in terms of *structural* sameness: all are ultimately a result of some sort of isomorphism. Universality is thereby not a matter of similarity but rather one of *identity*, namely an identity of structure. In the order of explanation, there is thus ultimately only one fundamental ground or base of universality, namely *structure* or—as Plato was to call it—*form* (*eidos*). In the final analysis even phenomenal universals such as colors have their origin and basis in structural uniformity. And while objects are always unique structures are inherently repeatable. To be sure, the concept of structure—of patterns and forms of order—covers a considerably varied terrain, seeing that there are not only spatial but also temporal, which is to say processual structures. And throughout nature every form of being—physical, chemical, biological, social—exhibits its own structures and thereby responds to the structure of others. Our understanding of universals roots in the mind's capacity to discern and reidentify the features of lawful order manifest in the world about us.

NOTES FOR CHAPTER 5

[1] Sive subsistant, sive in solis nudis intellectibus posita sint, sive subsistentia corporalia an incorporalia, et utrum separata a sensibilbus posita an circa haec consistentia.

NOTES FOR CHAPTER 5

[2] There is also a different sense of realism—one whose contrast is not *nominalism/conceptionalism*, but rather one whose contrast is *idealism*. In this sense of the term items whose dependency status is G or H are seen in a realistic light and those whose dependency status is I or H or S are viewed in an idealistic light. The traditional quarrel relates to the status of the objects at issue in human (and by extension in scientific) experience. Realism seen then in the former manner as independent of intelligence and intelligent beings, idealism see them as mind-dependent. (The operative motto here is "to be is to be conceived".)

Chapter 6

AQUINAS AND THE PRINCIPLE OF EPISTEMIC DISPARITY

1. THE PRINCIPLE OF EPISTEMIC DISPARITY

There can be no doubt that ignorance exacts a price in incomprehension. And here it is instructive to consider this circumstance theological light.

The world we live in is a manifold that is not of our making but of Reality's—or of God's if you will. And the Old Testament is strikingly explicit on these matters: For what is now at issue might be called *Isaiah's Principle* on the basis of the verse:

> For My thoughts are not your thoughts, neither are your ways My way, says the Lord. For as the heavens are higher than the Earth, so are My ways higher than your ways, and My thoughts than your thoughts. [Isaiah 55: 8-9.]

And again:

> Who has plumbed the mind of the Lord. What man can tell Him His plan? ... His wisdom cannot be fathomed [Isaiah 40: 15?-28.]

Christian theologians have often proceed along the same line of thought, as in clear in the teachings of St. Thomas Aquinas. He writes:

> The knowledge that is natural to us has its source in our senses and therefore extends just as far as it can be led by sensible things. But our understanding cannot reach to an apprehension of God's essence from these. (S. T., *Questions on God*, Q. 12, § 12.)

A fundamental law of epistemology is at work here namely what might be called the Principle of Epistemic Disparity to the effect that *a mind of lesser power is for this very reason unable to understand adequately the workings of a mind of greater power.* An intellect that can only just manage to play tic-tac-toe cannot possibly comprehend the ways of one that is expert at chess. To be sure, the weaker mind can doubtless realize *that* the stronger can solve problems it itself cannot. But it cannot understand *how* it manages to do so. The knowledge of limited knowers is inevitably restricted in matters of detail. To the lesser mind the performances of a more powerful one are bound to seem like magic.

Consider in this light the vast disparity of computational power between a mathematical tyro like most of us and a mathematical prodigy like Ramanujan. Not only cannot our tyro manage to answer the number-theoretic questions that such a genius resolves in the blink of an eye, but the tyro cannot even begin to understand the processes and procedures that the Indian genius employs. As far as the tyro is concerned, it is all sheer wizardry. No doubt once an answer is given he can check its correctness. But actually finding the answer is something which that lesser intellect cannot manage—the how of the business lies beyond its grasp. And, for much the same sort of reason, a mind of lesser power cannot discover what the question-resolving limits of a mind of greater power are. It can never say with warranted assurance where the limits of question-resolving power lie. (In some instances it may be able to say what's in and what's out, but never map the dividing boundary). And it is not simply that a more powerful mind will know quantitatively more facts than a less powerful one, but that its conceptual machinery is ampler in encompassing ideas and issues that are quantitatively inaccessible in lying altogether outside the conceptual horizon of its less powerful compeers.

Now insofar as the relation of a lesser towards a higher intelligence is replaced in analogous parallelism in to the relation between an earlier state of science and a later state. It is not that Aristotle could not have comprehended quantum theory—he was a very smart fellow and could certainly have learned. But what he could not have done it to formulate quantum theory within his own conceptual framework, his own familiar terms of reference. The very ideas at issue lay outside of the conceptual horizon of Aristotle's science, and like present-day students he would have had to master them from the ground up. Just this sort of thing is at issue with the relation of a less powerful intelligence to a more powerful one. It has been said insightfully that from the vantage point of a less developed technology another, substantially advanced technology is indistinguishable from magic. And exactly the same holds for a more advanced *conceptual* (rather than physical) technology.

It is instructive to contemplate in this light the hopeless difficulties encountered nowadays in the popularization of physics—of trying to characterize the implications of quantum theory and relativity theory for cosmology into the subscientific language of everyday life. A classic *obiter dictum* of Niels Bohr is relevant: "We must be clear that, when it comes to atoms, language can be used only as in poetry." And so, alas, we have to recognize that in philosophy, too, we are in the final analysis in something of the same position. In the history of culture, Homo sapiens began his quest for knowledge in the realm of poetry. And in the end it seems that in basic respect we are destined to remain close to this starting point.

The principle at issue with the general epistemic disparity between lesser and larger intellects is not something that St. Thomas articulated *expressis verbis*, in so many words. He was, however, perfectly clear regarding the limitations of finite minds in relation to God and perfectly aware of the crucial distinction between the *that* of things on the one hand and the *what* and *how* of things on the other. Citing the authority of Dionysius,[1] he agrees that "things of a higher order cannot be known through likenesses of a uniform order" (S. T., Q. 12, art. 3), so that "God's essence is unfathomable [to us], combining to a transcended degree whatever can be signified or understood by a created mind" (loc. cit.) All in all, then, the salient point of man/God disparity is one that Aquinas grasps with admissible precision:

2. A PARADOX AND ITS RESOLUTION

A paradox seems to emerge in this connection. On the one hand we are told that we cannot fathom the mind of God. On the other hand we are given all sorts of information about it: that it is omniscient, that it knows truths by immediate insight, that it does not proceed discursively, etc. Indeed whole chapters of the *Summa* is dedicated to God's knowledge (viz. Question 14). How can this seeming conflict be resolved?

Let us ask St. Thomas. He tells us:

Whoever sees God in his essence sees something that exists infinitely, and sees it to be infinitely intelligent, but without understanding it infinitely. It is as thought one might realize *that* a certain proposition can be proved without realizing *how* one can to this. (S. T., Q. 12, art. 7.)

As is usual in philosophy—and was virtually universal in medieval philosophy—the problem is solved by means of distinctions. And with characteristic acumen, Aquinas puts his finger upon exactly the right distinction, namely that between *product* and *process*. Quite in general, we know THAT God can do all sorts of things, while nevertheless lacking any and all information as to just HOW this is managed. For instance we know *that* God is omniscient without having any clue as to *how* he goes about it.

Yet another crucial distinction also comes into it, namely that between positivity and negativity—as St. Thomas clearly recognizes. All of those things we know about God's mind are actually negative in their bearing.

- God is omniscient: that is, there is no fact that he fails to know.

- God's knowledge is immediate: that is, it is nowise discursive or inferential.

- God's knowledge is exact: that is, it is nowise approximate or imprecise

In characterizing God we have little alternative but to use the *via negativa* because the entire terminology at our disposal regarding matters of mundane applicability does not—cannot—extend to God. And Aquinas emphatically endorsed the thesis of Diogenes that the terminology of ordinary usage does not pertain to God because "what they [ordinary words] signify does not belong to God in the way that they signify it, but in a higher way." (S. T., Q. 12 art. 13).

The ontological chasm that separates the finite and the infinite means that a terminology that accommodates concepts devised to accommodate the cognitive needs of the former cannot be employed literally in relation to the latter.

3. LESSONS

Are there any significant lessons to be drawn from the theologian's doctrine of an epistemic disparity between men and God by those philosophers who are not theologically engaged—those who are atheistic or agnostic or simply reluctant to invoke God in philosophical deliberations? I do believe that there are and they run somewhat as follows.

In characterizing the universe as designed intelligently we deal only with the product and not the means of its realization. It is one thing to consider the universe as designed *by an intelligence* and quite another to think it to be designed *intelligently*. After all, the feature of an item is one thing and the manner of its production another. (A house can be gigantic without having been built by giants.) To say that nature is so constituted *as though* a supreme intelligence had designed it is no more theistically committal than to say that a river's course proceeds as though a palsied cartographer had planned it is anthropomorphically committal. Both modes of expression in fact merely describe the nature of the product and actually remain silent on the means of its production. To be designed intelligently is one thing—namely to exhibit intelligence IN design—but to be designed BY intelligence is something else again. To say that Nature comports itself rationally—that its modus operandi is so constituted *as though* it were the product of a creative intelligence—is to be *descriptive* and not *explanatory* about it.

So let it be granted—at least for the sake of discussion that—prescinding entirely from the issue of its productive origin—we exist in a world that exhibits complexity, subtlety, and coherence to a degree that we can plausibly deem it as intelligently contrived. And now let us contemplate the *purely hypothetical* question: "If (even though contrary to your belief) this universe whose intelligent design you have conceded were to be the product of a creative designer, then would not this creator have to be of an intelligence vastly more powerful than that which we knowers can claim for ourselves—be it individually or collectively?" Clearly, the intelligent design of such a world sets the bar so high that we could not actually meet it. And so, given the almost inevitably affirmative answer to our purely hypothetical question, the Principle of Epistemic Disparity immediately comes into operation to indicate that in the final analysis we really cannot expect to achieve a fully and definitively adequate understanding of the modus operandi of nature.

Against this background, then, the Principle of Epistemic Disparity strongly suggests that there may indeed be a limit to the extent to which we humans can realize the aspiration of achieving a final theory that comprehensively accounts for the endlessly vast tapestry of the phenomena of nature. And consequently, while there is no problem with the idea of *improving* our scientific understanding of the world, nevertheless the idea of *perfecting* it must be rejected as an unattainable pie in the sky. In science as elsewhere, coming to the end of *our* road does not necessarily mean coming to the end of *the* road.

And so the lesson of these deliberations—even for those caught up in the unhappy state of *odium theologicum*—is given in a paraphrase of Hamlet: "There are more things in heaven and earth, Horatio, than are dreamt of in your science."[2]

NOTES FOR CHAPTER 6

[1]   *The Devine Names* 4, IV, G. 3.588.

[2]   This chapter constitutes an address given by the author on the occasion of the award of the Aquinas Medal of the American Catholic Philosophical Association in Milwaukee in October of 2007.

Chapter 7

SELF-SUBSTANTIATING STATEMENTS

1. SELF SUBSTANTIATION

Every statement[1] gives rise to two semantically related families of further statements:

(1) Its *assertoric consequences*: those statements that will hold if it does—those which, *according to it*, will have to be true on the supposition that it is.

(2) Its *meta-descriptors*: those statements *about* it that are true through stating or following from features characterizing that statement itself.

Thus the statement "Magnets attract iron" has as one of its assertonic consequences "Something attracts iron", but it further figures among its meta-descriptions that this statement itself is universal, affirmative, and about iron, so that we have:

- "Magnets attract iron" is a universal statement.

- "Magnets attract iron" is an affirmative statement.

- "Magnets attract iron" is a statement about iron.

None of these three statements is affirmed or *asserted by* "Magnets attract iron", but all of them are *true about* this statement.

However, in certain cases a particular proposition will *both* figure among the assertoric consequences of a statement *and also* among its meta-descriptors. Thus consider the statement

(*S*) "All statements make intelligible assertions."

And now consider the cognate statement

- "(*S*) makes an intelligible assertion."

This statement is at once an assertoric consequence of (*S*) and a meta-descriptive claim that is true about it. (It is, of course, questionable whether (*S*) itself is true, but that is irrelevant to the matter under consideration.)

However, a self-substantiating statement is one such that *this very statement itself* also figures among its own meta-descriptions. Thus consider the statement:

(*A*) This statement is affirmative.

Since (*A*) is itself an affirmative proposition, it follows that "(*A*) is affirmative" is a meta-descriptor of (*A*). And it is also, of course, just what it itself claims. Accordingly (*A*) is not only self-instantiating but also self-substantiating.

Moreover, consider the statement

- This statement is not affirmative.

It is, clearly, a meta-truth about this statement that it is *not* affirmative. Since *this self-engendered fact entails the very statement at issue*, this statement is also self-substantiating.

Some further typical instances of self-substantiating statements are as follows:

- This (statement) is a statement.

- This statement claims the existence of something (viz. a statement).

- This is a statement about statements.

- This statement is not self-contradictory.

- This statement logically entails many others.

In this way a statement will be self-substantiating or self-confirmatory if there are true facts *about* that statement which entail what it asserts—facts from which that statement itself follows. With such a statement the facts brought to realization by that statement's being what it is suffice to ensure that the statement itself is true (i.e., suffice as an information basis for the deduction of that statement).

2. ISSUES OF NECESSITY

The statement

- "This statement exists."

is clearly both true and self-substantiating. And the truth of "Some statements exist" is accordingly necessitated.
But is the existence of statements really necessary?
It turns on how we construe the idea of a "statement". If we were dealing with abstract propositions, then the proposition:

- This proposition is true.

would indeed be true and true of necessity since no matters of contingent existence are involved. But if—as we have stipulated here—statements are linguistically formulated propositions, then the existence of statements depends on the existence of languages—and this, so we may suppose, is a matter of contingent fact. Merely to *specify* a proposition is to ensure its *existence*—though not, of course, its *truth* since the state of affairs at issue can be merely possible rather than actual. However for a *statement* to exist as such it has to be made: a statement must, as such, be given linguistic embodiment. Were the no languages there would be no statements, though propositions, being correlative with mere possibilities, would still exist.
A self-substantiating statement on the order of

- This statement is affirmative.

deserves to be classified (1) as *a priori* rather than as *a posteriori* because no experience over and above an understanding of the statement itself is needed for its verification, (2) as *analytic* rather than *synthetic* because merely linguistic information suffices to establish its truth, (3) as necessary.
Let us examine this last point more closely. Consider the following statement

A | This is the only statement, made in Box A

What this statement says is certainly true. But nevertheless the statement is not self-substantiating because its substantiation requires information over and above what that statement itself affords—namely information about the contexts of Box A. The statement "This statement can be translated into Polish" is in the same boat in that its depiction requires information beyond what it itself provides.[2]

By contrast, consider the statement

•   "This statement claims P."

Clearly what this statement says about itself (viz. that it claims P [or that $2 + 2 = 4$]) is not only true but has that statement itself as a logical consequence. Accordingly the statement is self-substantiating—and is so irrespective of what P says and indeed even irrespective of P's truth.

And just this will of course hold for all self-substantiating statements. For if what the statements claims to be so with regard to itself is indeed a feature that it does actually exhibit, then this circumstance automatically establishes its truth. In this way, a self-substantiating statement is one whose very make up suffices to ensure its truth.

The phenomenon of self-certification illustrates that some such statements are caught up in self-reference in a way that renders them automatically true because they themselves provide material capable of establishing what is being claimed. In effect, these self substantive statements are statements claiming that "This statement has the feature F" when this very statement itself indeed possesses the feature in question. Such statements are always true and indeed necessarily so.

Consider the statement

•   "This statement asserts that P [say that $2 + 2 = 4$]."

Clearly this statement is self-substantiatingly true, seeing that what it asserts is incontestably the case. Accordingly, such statements are true of necessity.

But is the necessity at issue absolute and categorical, or is it merely conditional? Clearly the former. What a statement says may well be contingent but *that it says* so is unconditionally necessary. For consider the statement

- "This statement could assert something different from what it does."

That this statement asserts what it does is (logico-conceptually) necessary, being essential to its very identity. But what it asserts is clearly absurd. The statements could not assert something other than what they do assert because if (*per impossibile*) a statement asserted something different from what it actually does, then it would not be the same statement that it actually is, so that the requisite move to "this statement" would be precluded.

The lesson of these deliberations is that we have little choice but to see the status of self-substantiating statements to be not only that of truth but of *logico-conceptually necessary* truth.

Since self-substantive statements are necessary truths it follows that they are logically consistent with any self-consistent proposition. But now let S be any such statement, and consider the statement

- "This statement is (logically) comparable with S."

Any statement answering to this schema is bound to be self-certifying. This at once assures an infinitude of self-certifying truths.

One can, of course, move inferentially from "This statement has the features F & G" to "This G-featuring statement has the feature F". And now one can move on to "Some G-featuring statements have the feature F". Thus for the self-substantiating statement "This [affirmative] statement is about statements" we can infer "Some affirmative statements are about statements". But while that statement follows from its self-substantiating predecessor it is not itself self-substantiating.

3. SOME POINTS OF LOGIC

Any statement of the format "This statement if F" allows for an automatic transit along the line

this (statement) $\rightarrow$ some (statements) $\rightarrow$ there are statements

Accordingly we can move from "This statement is affirmative" to "Some statements are affirmative" to "There are affirmative statements". All such variants spread the web of self-substantiation yet more widely. However we cannot go quite so far as

- "This statement is true."

For this statement does not automatically instantiate itself and so does not supply the materials for envisioning its own truth. To move in this direction, we would have to go on to take the further step endorsing it as true (which it could, quite plausibly, be seen as not being).

Consider the difference between

(1) Some statements have the feature F [where this feature actually characterizes this statement itself].

and

(2) This statement has the feature F.

Here statement 2 of course entails statement 1. But clearly statement 1 does not entail statement 2 in the absence of that parenthetical addendum. We have a one-way entailment and not a reciprocal equivalency.

The salient fact here is that the substance of that crucial parenthetical addendum is something that statement 1 *exhibits* but does not *state*. (Unlike statement 2 which does both.) Self-substantiating statements accordingly afford a paradigmatic illustration for Ludwig Wittgenstein's Tractarian distinction between a statement's *stating* and its *manifesting* some feature, between showing (*zeigen*) and affirming (*sagen*).[3]

The salient generic feature of self-substantiating statements are as follows:

- They must be self-referential statements.

- They must be particular, since as specific propositions they cannot provide for generality.

- They must be about statements (since they are about themselves).

- They must ascribe to themselves a feature that they themselves possess.

- They are bound to be true.

In relation to the second consider the statement:

- "All statements are about something."

Though true enough. But its very generality precludes it from being true by virtue of self-substantiation. It is self-illustrating but not self-substantiating.

There is, accordingly, no limit to the range of self-substantiating statements. To see this, note that various sorts of things hold by logical necessity for all statements (for example: "For all p: $p \supset p$."). In such cases we have:

For all p: $\vdash Fp$

that F is a logically universal feature of meaningful statements. Now consider the contention

- "This statement has the feature F."

It will obtain on logical grounds alone that this statement is F (since all statements are). But, since that is exactly what the statement itself claims, it is self-substantiating. In a way then, all self-certifying statements will honor the laws of proportional logic, all of which take the form: For all p, Fp.

4. MATTERS OF SUBSTITUTION

A statement of the format:

(S) "This statement is F"

or

S is F

gives rise to the following substantiation series by way of progress

"This statement is F" is F or: $(S$ is $F)$ is F

"'This statement is F' is F" is F or: $((S$ is $F)$ is $F)$ is F

etc.

Now if S is F is indeed true, then this will also hold for the entire series of progressive reiterations. In this way, every self-substantiating statement inaugurates an infinite series of further elaborators whose nature is such that if one is true, all the others are bound to be so.

But how is the claim at issue in the original statement to be viewed in relation to the progressive substitution sequence to which it gives rise? There are three prime possibilities here:

1. *Expansively* as a (tacit rather than explicit) abbreviation of the entire sequence itself.

2. *Conjunctively* as a (tacit rather than explicit) abbreviation for the infinite conjunction of this sequence's members.

3. *Compactly* as self-sufficiently complete by itself while giving rise to the other members of the sequence only inferentially, even as a statement p stands self-sufficient on its own, while yet giving rise to $p \vee x$, $(p \vee x) \vee x$, etc. only inferentially (where x is some self-contradictory proposition so that all member of the sequence are equivalent.

Alternatives 1 and 2 run into problems with the seeming truth of "This statement can be formulated in English in fewer than twenty words". It thus seems sensible to adopt Alternative 3.

Be this as it may, the reality of it is that the statement-descriptive qualifiers F at issue as self-descriptive truth of the format "This statement is F" can be classified into three groups:

1. *The omnipresent* which will obtain throughout the entire substitution sequence. Example: *is affirmative* (or *is negative*, or *concerns being*.

2. *The inaugurating* which holds only of the first member of the sequence. Example: *contains one single verb.*

3. *The expiring* which will hold only up to a certain point. Example: *can be stated in ten seconds.*

Omnipresent descriptive statement-qualifiers—and they alone—will hold good irrespective of how a self-referential statement is interpreted (whether omnipresently or inauguratingly or expiringly).

Some logicians and semantical theorists have been wont to rule out all self-referential statements as inappropriate and meaningless. Now to be sure, some self-referential statements will indeed prove to be self-contradictory: "This statement is false" for example, or "All general statements admit of exceptions." Nevertheless, to take this line is to throw out the baby with the bath water. In logic as in domestic management allowing a few bad apples to condemn the whole barrel of rejection is taking matters too far. For as we have seen, at least one class of self-referring statements—viz., those which are self-substantiating—are to all visible appearances not only meaningful but indeed true, and arguably even necessarily so.[4]

NOTES FOR CHAPTER 7

[1] For present purposes a pivotal distinctions must be drawn, namely between

  • *a state of affairs* (the cat's being on the mat.)

  • *a proposition* (the idea or conception that a certain possible state of affairs obtains, e.g., the idea or conception that the cat is on the mat).

  • *a statement* (the formulation of a proposition in a particular language, e.g. "Die Katze ist auf der Matte.").

States of affairs need not be actual, they can be merely possible as well. Nor need statements be true. Moreover, note that many statements can formulate the same proposition, and many propositions can correctly characterize a given state of affairs.

[2] To be sure, if we contemplate a larger body of "background information" to provide premisses additional to the information of the statement itself, then the range

NOTES FOR CHAPTER 7

of its meta-descriptions will expand. For example, "This statement is made in English" will achieve self-substantiation when we suppose (as we can hardly avoid doing!) what it is for a statement to be made in English.

[3] Ludwig Wittgenstein, *Tractatus Logico-Philosophicus*, sect. 4.022.

[4] I am indebted to Anil Gupta for constructive comments on a draft of this chapter.

Chapter 8

REGRET

1. WHAT REGRET INVOLVES

Regret is in order whenever one acts suboptimally. And the human condition being what it is, this fact plays a prominent role in life—and in literature as well, with Judas Iscariot standing at the head of the pack, closely followed by Shakespeare's *Othello*.

Je ne regrette rien, "I regret nothing," goes the infamous song of the famous French chanteuse Edith Piaf. But the agent who never does anything regrettable—that is, *deserving* of regret—is an angel rather than a human being. And the human who never regrets what he does is a self-satisfied prig—and a decidedly wicked one at that. The realistic circumstances of human life are such that doing regrettable things is effectively inevitable.

"Never do anything you'll regret!" just is not a viable piece of advice given the imperfection of human foreknowledge. Those lost opportunities that run afoul of this injunction are all too often viable only with the wisdom of hindsight. The circumstances of life in this "vale of tears" being what they are, regret is bound to play a prominent role in human affairs.

Regretting the loss of opportunity for realizing a positive result is a familiar occurrence, and dismay at having missed a chance is a common and appropriate form of regret. On the opposite side, a positive glow of pleasure is likely to accompany the realization that a foregone opportunity involves missing out on a loss.

To understand what regret is we do well to begin by looking at how the relevant terminology is standardly used. And here a crucial distinction stands in the foreground, namely that between:

- *personal regret* of the sort at issue with the locution "*X* regrets".

and

- *impersonal regret* of the sort at issue with the locution "It is regrettable that".

Personal regret is typified by that ex-printer Benjamin Franklin's contemplation of the *errata* in his life, the things he wishes it were possible to erase and re-write in the account of his life-story. It consists in contemplating and in some measure lamenting "the road not taken". One can, of course, regret not only something that one has done but also something that one has failed to do. There are regrets of commission and regrets of omission—of lamenting one's fault in regard to "the one that got away" through a failure of timely action on one's part.

German distinguishes sharply between personal remorse-style regret (*es tut mir Leid*) and impersonal, negativity assessment style regret (*ich bedauere es dass*) of the sort at issue with the English locution "It is regrettable that [he had an accident]". This second is effectively tantamount to, "It is unfortunate that ..." and is purely evaluative, a matter of the negative assessment of some occurrence, solution, or state of affairs. The intention and causal activity of an agent is not at issue here—though of course it may well be that it is the regretter's own fat that is in the fire. The last German Kaiser and the protagonist of W. S. Maugham's *Of Human Bondage* no doubt regretted their physical deformity—i.e., deemed it regrettable. But of course the failure of personal responsibility does not come into it in such cases which pivot on what one *is* rather than what one *does*. Personal regret relates specifically to making mistakes. The locution "You'll live to regret that" is either a monitory prediction offering good counsel, or else an actual threat that omits prefixing a tacit "The foreseeable course of events (if not I myself) will see to it that ..."

Regret is not an unalloyed negativity. For there is, in the end, a bright side to regret as well. After all, regret both exhibits and develops characters—one knows a good deal about a person when one knows about the actions and omissions that have occasioned him (or her) regret. For regret exhibits where the heart is. (This is why in declining an invitation one is supposed to "send one's regrets".)

There certainly are such circumstances as regret-dilemmas, where, do-it-or-not regret is bound to eventuate either way. You are destined for regret either way—damned if you do, and damned if you don't. The poet's lament:

I could have been happy with either
Were't other dear charmer away

illustrates this.

Institutional regret is a closer to impersonal than to personal regret in that it does not involve the elements of responsibility and remorse. "H. M. Government regrets that your representative has misinterpreted its intention" has the form "*X* regrets" alright but puts the aspect of agent-responsibility aside.

2. RAMIFICATIONS OF REGRET

Can one regret something that someone else has done? Can I regret that you have offended your brother or that Hitler invaded Poland? These are certainly things I can lament and deem regrettable. But it hardly makes sense to speak of personal regret here because the element of responsibility is absent. The only things I can regret in this sense of the term as those for whose occurrence (or nonoccurrence) I feel myself to have some degree of personal responsibility. The aspect of "it's my own fault" is pivotal here, so that when one regrets something there is an inclination to "kick oneself". Accordingly, personal regret is not just lamentation—not just reflecting on how unfortunate it is that something or other negative is the case—but combining this with the painful realization that this unfortunate eventuation has come to realization at least partially through an action or omission of one's own, so that one bears (at least in part) the burden of responsibility for the negativity at issue.

Personal regret is accordingly predicated on the belief or conviction that:

If only I had done *X* (as I indeed could and should have done), then the result which counted certainly or probably or at least possibly have ensued would be significantly better (or at least nowise as bad) as that [result] which has in fact occurred.

As this analysis indicates, regret is predicated on a conviction (1) in the reality of free agency (2) in the causal efficacy of action, and (3) in the evaluative status of states of affairs.

Seen in this light, personal regret is the natural response to being faced with the unpalatable and unasked-for consequences of one's own actions. It is a matter of wishing that something or other one had done (or left undone) were of the opposite condition because one believes that its being as is has contributed to the realization of an unfavorable result. The inventory of the sorts of things that involve personal fault-assumption regret is long:

moral and ethical transgressions, social gaffes, sloppy workmanship, mistakes and blades of immeasurable costs, the list is endless.

Personal regret clearly has many occasions. It may be a response to damage to one's character through moral ethical transgression (loss of self-worth), or to damage to one's standing through social or cultural faux pas (loss of face), or of loss to economic standing either by aide diminution or by sacrificing the chance for their improvement. In any case personal regard always addresses some sort of personal loss—that is simply how the concept works.

Regret usually involves self-reproach—but not always. I may regret not having bought a lottery ticket—after all, I might have won. But this is not something I can sensibly *reproach* myself for. In *such* cases regret should be accompanied by remorse or even shame, which is when the issue is one of a negative result that has befallen someone else due to one's own deliberate agency. Here the agent's emotions ought properly to be engaged by way of self-recrimination and self-reproach (ideally accompanied by a determination to make proper amends). Remorse thus calls for apology, compensation, and damage control. It is specifically the personal be-sorry-that rather than the impersonal deem unfortunate style of regret—that which invokes responsibility assumption and self-reproach—which will be at issue here. Of course, remorse is only rationally appropriate where one "could have done otherwise".

An agent's act of omission or commission can be undeservedly detrimental to the interests of another either positivity (by producing some sort of damage or injury) or negativity (by failing to engender a result that could be beneficial)—that is, it can be either harmful or unhelpful. If I blackmail X into putting gall in your soup, I act on the former way; if I decline lending you the fare for a projected journey I act in the latter way. The fact invariably calls for regret—and indeed also for apology, remorse, and amends; the latter need not evoke this sort of response. The overall situation with regard to regret is summarized in Display 1.

3. MEASURING REGRET

Personal regret can be measured in terms of "the difference it has made". It is a matter of the gap between "what happened when I did" and "what could reasonably be expected to have happened if I had acted otherwise".

R = (value of the net expectable outcome had the agent acted otherwise)

—(value of the actual outcome)

The first (quantitative) factor represents *gross* regret, the overall quantity is *net* regret.

Consider an example. You offer me (at the cost of $ 10) a 50:50 chance of winning $ 50. I decline. Had I invested $ 10, the expected value of the gamble was $ 25 so that the expectable profit is $ 25 – $ 10 = $15. In actuality I have neither gain nor loss so the value of the actual outcome is $ 0. The overall net regret value of the case is thus $ 15 – $ 0 = $ 15.

On this basis there will of course be such a thing as *negative* regret. The English language affords no exact word for this factor. Perhaps *unregret* might be made to serve. Thus in the preceding example if the charge had been $ 30 (instead of $ 10) for entering into the gamble at issue then the regret for not having done so would have been valued at $ 25 – $30 = –$ 5. This sum would, in the circumstances, measure the value of the unregret that accrues from not chancing the gamble.

4. MALFUNCTIONING OF REGRET

There can be no personal regret without personal of responsibility. Personal regret is coordinate with agency, and in situations of personal regret an agent takes the line that there is:

1. *productive responsibility* in part or whole for something that is a matter of

2. *negative evaluation* because the focal situation at issue is unfortunate.

3. *counterfactual supposition*: "if only I (or X) had not done A then that negative result R would/might not have occurred.

4. *Counteractual wishing*; "would I had acted differently."

Without these three factors of productivity, negativity, and counterfactuality personal regret with its counteractual wishing would be inappropriate.

Thus consider:

Productive responsibility. Suppose I regret having eaten the pie which (so I think) caused the stomach upset that kept me up all night. But in fact it was the spoiled mayonnaise on the hard boiled eggs that caused the problem. The causal mis-diagnosis has rendered my regret inappropriate. Even if I had not eaten the pie, I would have had the stomach upset anyhow.

Evaluation. I give you as present a picture from my attic that I deemed worthless. And as I reflect on this, I regret it—you deserved better of me. But in actual fact it actually was a rare old master painting—I had mis-evaluated that picture completely. It is thus clear that here my regret is seriously defective.

Counterfactual supposition. Suppose I regret having shot my enemy to death (so I think). In fact I pumped the bullet into a corpse—the victim of a recent heart attack. Now we have to be careful. I regret having *killed* him—and that regret is quite inappropriate: I didn't. But if, instead, I were to regret having *shot* him (or having *tried* to kill him).

Wishing. Even if I deem a result as positive, if I do not wish for it, then my failure in relation to its realization is not a source of regret.

Accordingly, an agent proceeds incorrectly in regard to regret when he thinks:

—that he has done something which he actually did not do but just mis-remembers.

—that which he has done has had certain misfortunate effects which it actually did not have at all.

—that if only he had proceeded otherwise a more positive result would have ensued, whereas in fact things would have turned out even more badly.

Display 1

THE TAXONOMY OF REGRET

A   B

The agent feels dismay (distress)   *And this negativity*
at some negativity that   *is something for whose*
                                      happening the agent himself
(1) has happened
                                      (1) bears some responsibility
(2) has happened to oneself
                                      (2) bears no responsibility
(3) has happened to others

The concept of *impersonal regret* encompasses all of cases A1, A2, A3.
The concept of *personal regret* covers cases A1 + B1, A2 + B1, A2 + B1,
thus including all cases where B1 is at issue. The concept of *remorse* covers case A3 + B1.

Deliberations about regret will certainly have to take account of the difference between appropriate and inappropriate regret.

Can one reasonably regret doing something that has produced a good
result? A positive response is clearly in order. For suppose my action is
such that one would ordinarily regret its expectable outcome, while nevertheless contrary-to-expectation a good outcome has accidentally ensued. I
rob you of the cash you would otherwise have used to book a ticket on a
flight that crashes. Here regret for my wrongdoing is perfectly in order and
the benign upshot nowise cancels out the reprehensibility of my immoral
act. Thus I can, quite appropriately regret my transgression in having
committed a robbery, though of course I cannot and should not regret the
result of my misdeed (viz., that it has inadvertently saved your life).

Is personal regret rationally in order when the unfortunate result that ensued from one's action is something that could not possibly have been
foreseen because it involves a fluke of some sort? Here a negative response
is called for. Regret is only warranted (sensible, rationally appropriate)

when one's proceeding is open to mental reproach—that is when one could reasonably be expected to have foreseen the prospect of unfortunate consequences of what one has done.

Man is not infallible—most of what we do can go amiss, regret included. And with regret in particular, all sorts of "human error" is possible. And so, ironically, there is even room for regret with respect to regret.

Consider the objection:

Regret makes no sense. For it is predicated on the idea that one would have done otherwise. And this is systematically mistaken. We do what we must.

This objection is based upon the problematic and almost certainly erroneous fatalism—the idea that people's actions are foreshadowed and that the idea that we could have acted otherwise is always and unavoidably mistaken. If we see ourselves as free rational agents—as it is only right and proper to do—then regret must, on not infrequent occasion—be an altogether proper and appropriate course for us.

5. IS REGRET RATIONAL?

Is personal regret rational? Does it ever make good sense to regret something? It might seem that regret is futile. After all, the past cannot be undone. As Omar Kayyam said: "Not all thy piety nor wit, can bring it back to cancel half a line."

To regret something is to function in the realm of evaluation and judgment: regret makes sense only when an outcome is adjudged negatively, and such an evaluation will only be warranted when the agent has (or at least *takes* himself to have) good reasons for so proceeding.

The rational appropriateness of regret is a function of just what it is that is being regretted. The point is that personal regret is something that transpires in the mind of an agent. And this agent can be wrong regarding the essentials of the matter.

What then of the dictum: "No use crying over spilled milk." Surely, so this will insist, it is altogether futile to wish we could undo the past? Is this sort of thing not a waste of time, attention, energy, and effort in fretting about what can't be helped?

However the answer here is negative. Regret is not futile. First of all, it can lay the motivational foundation for better behavior in the future. And moreover, it is a useful instrumentality of character formation, seeing that regret of a misdeed is by its very nature something morally laudable. The capacity and indeed tendency to regret one's misdeeds is a significant part of what makes one human. (This is one of the many useful lessons of the Bible's Garden-of-Eden story.)

Regret would be generally and universally inappropriate if:

(1) People's freely chosen actions and omissions never made a difference to actions simply because no action or omission of people are ever free, so that a condition of universal fatalism obtains.

(2) Evaluation is never justified: good/bad, desirable/undesirable, and all such like evaluation rest on illusion and misunderstanding.

(3) Wishing for that which is not—either generally or at least in relation to human actions—is always futile and inappropriate.

And so as long as one is not a fatalist neither a value-nihilist nor a rock-ribbed realist, one cannot but hold the view that regret can, on occasion, be proper and appropriate. For regret can serve to provide a basis of understanding and instruction for a determination to do better in the future. In crying over spilled milk we create a measurable experience that serves as an ongoing reminder to be careful when carrying milk henceforward. And moreover, it can serve to develop and strengthen a commitment to positive and constructive proceedings.

6. IS REGRET MORAL?

Regret can have a merely prudential bearing. (I can regret not taking advantage of a bargain.) Sometimes but not always—for it is bound to have a moral dimension where the interests of others are concerned.

It is effectively axiomatic that the failure to regret a morally reprehensible action or omission is itself morally reprehensible. The criminal may regret his crime alright, but this may well occur only when caught—and even then may be directed at letting himself be caught rather than at the crime itself. In regret situations where the interests of others are involved, remorse becomes a moral imperative.

What is one to say of the individual who regrets inappropriately—who regrets something that is not inherently regret-deserving or fails to regret something that is in fact regrettable? The first person is clearly being foolish. But the second person is in a worse boat yet—not merely foolish but contemptible. For in failing to regret something that actually calls for it we are being heedless when only our own interests are at stake and outright immoral when the interests of others are.

Regret in and of itself is ethically neutral. It is all a matter of what is regretted. Regretting a deliberation a misdeed is morally mandatory—and should indeed be unlamented by way of apologizing and compensation. On the other hand, regret at the loss of an opportunity for malice or mischief is socially reprehensible. To be sure, what matters from the moral point of view is not just regret but also its exact object. The evaluation of regret is very much a matter of the sort of thing that is being regretted. A failure to regret having done something foolish is itself foolish, and a failure to regret having done something wicked is itself wrong—as would be the regret of a lost opportunity for doing something wicked.

The moral standing of so acting as to make someone regret something they would otherwise not have regretted is decidedly variable. The hardened criminal may regret his crime only because he is caught and punished—and in this case causing him regret is clearly a good thing. On the other hand, if I lead you to regret your meeting with me by means of a gratuitous insult, this is something bad. The point is that in the second case you have done nothing regret-worthy while that hardened criminal indeed has. Engendering regret in someone is nothing good or bad in itself—it all depends on the nature of the circumstances.

And regret certainly admits of doubt. A World War I companion in arms of Adolf Hitler's may well regret his not having him in the back on the battlefield and yet acknowledge the moral turpitude of such committing such an act well before Hitler's demonic turn.

7. WHY REGRET IS PHILOSOPHICALLY RELEVANT

The overall lesson of these deliberations is that regret is inseparably coordinated with a certain view of ourselves and our place in the world's scheme of things. It is an (inherent) factor of the human condition as long as we deem ourselves to be free agents who can, must, and should act in this world with an imperfect knowledge of circumstance and situations—and thereby with incomplete control of the results and consequences of what we do.

Accordingly, various considerations conspire to render regret something that is relevant for philosophy, specifically including the following:

- Regret is a significant factor in rationality, being is something only rational agents can manage. But is it in fact rational ever to regret something?

- Regret is a significant factor in evaluation, since it is always based on the negative assessment of an outcome. But how is regret itself to be evaluated?

- Regret is a significant factor in the matters of free will, once it presupposes free agency. Does regretting an act make sense only if the agent at issue acted freely?

These considerations serve to establish and confirm the philosophical relevance and significance of this issue. For as such questions indicate, regret is inherently interconnected with philosophical issues of rationality, evaluation, morality and freedom of the will.

Chapter 9

THE PROBLEM OF EVIL

Evil comes in two forms: the physical evil inherent in pain and suffering, and the moral evil inherent in the wrongdoing of agents. Either way, evil is problematic. But the real problem of evil is not why there is evil in the world. There pretty much has to be some evil if any great good is to be realized. (Evil is effectively indispensable as a challenge to the good of its overcoming: there could be no triumph of good over evil if there were no evil in the world.) The prime problem is why there is so much of it.

On the side of moral evil then the key question is: "Why should it be that people are so immoral and cause so much suffering to one another?" The answer is not that hard to come by. It lies in the fact that mankind is a being whose will is free, whose intellect is limited, and whose disposition is selfish. The real problem lies elsewhere—with physical evil—a realm in which we may as well encompass the previous sentence's two latter considerations.

Of course physical evils are something else again. They are not due to the decisions and actions of willful men, but rather involve such things as plagues, diseases, accidents, earthquakes, floods, droughts, storms—not to speak of the ultimate tragedy of a mortality itself. They are inherent in the operations of nature. So it is here that the crux of the Problem of Evil seems to lie.

Only someone who does not see evil as an inevitable aspect of the real—someone who thinks that evil could not and should not be there—will see evil as problematic. A theorist who, like Plotinus or Schelling, sees physical evil as unavoidably inherent in the world's materiality need look no further for the explanation of physical evil. And determinists who deem the world as it is to be more of less inevitable—who think that things pretty much have to be the way they are—will also manage to sidestep "the Problem of Evil". The problem will confound only those who think (1) that things might be different and (2) that by rights they should be.

So, why so much evil? Now, quite in general, two key issues are posed by any question. First that of its presuppositions—*the background considerations* that render it problematic and explain how it arises. And second *the answer* that supposedly resolves it and affords its solution. As to the first, it is clear in our case that one can contemplate a considerable array of explanations for how it is that physical evil should exist even in a world regarded as the creative product of a benign God. They cover a wide spectrum ranging from the inevitably of evil in any inherently limited domain[1] to its positive function as a goad to human effort and occasion for the cultivation of virtue. But it is not this issue of *resolving* the Problem of Evil that will preoccupy us here. Our present concern, rather, will be with the issues at stake in *posing* the problem in the first place. So while the literature of the Problem of Evil for the most part addresses the issue of how the question is to be answered, the present discussion will focus on its presuppositions, and will accordingly consider what it is that makes the question into something significantly problematic in the first place.

The problem of Evil does not arise simply because the presence of evil in the world is unfortunate and evil is something bad. For this poses a *problem* only for someone who is convinced that *evil just should not be there*—that by rights bad things should not exist in the world because the *world ought to be a good place*. And just this sentiment—the ethico-normative idea that "by rights" the world should contain no evil—itself contains the core of a religious outlook because it embodies a commitment to the idea that the forces and processes that shape the world about us are somehow under an obligation to produce a good, user-friendly, benign world.

And so, the crux is this. Anyone who thinks that physical evil should not be there adopts an essentially ethical position toward the universe, subject to the idea of what it ought by rights to be like. But such a position only makes sense relative to the belief that there is an agency or agent that is responsible for the process of making the universe what it is and that this agent or agency is somehow obligated—i.e., owes it to us, to itself, or to whatever—to make this product as evil-free as possible. Absent such a belief the position makes no sense. But in accepting it an essentially theological stance is being adopted.

Only for someone committed to the ideas of a selectively functioning benevolent creator can the existence of evil in the world possibly constitute a problem; it is no problem for those who see it as part of the natural order of things—a *sine qua non* for existence as such. Or again, you think of reality as shaped by forces indifferent to good and evil—let alone as the product of forces that favor evil—then the presence of evil is not a problem for you at all. Only if you think of reality as the product of a benign agency—the work of a benevolent creator in specific—then alone will the world's evil become a real problem. Only someone who is a theist (badly construed) need be preoccupied about the problem of evil. The atheist has other things to worry about; for him the problem of evil disappears— reality is what it is, and that's that. With atheists the quest for the reason of things—for finding any rationality whatsoever in the real—becomes Quixotic: we can regret realities but cannot recriminate against them. The world's evil is a problem only for someone who believes that there is—or should be!—a somehow rational and responsible force at work in and on the world—one whose above operation is somehow at odds with the existence of evil.

Now the world's evils have been seen by many as an argument against the existence of God. (Think, for example, of Voltaire and the Lisbon earthquake of 1754.) They reason as follows:

- A benevolent God would not permit evil in a world of his creating.

- The world we live in is pervaded by evil.

Therefore: There is no benevolent God.

The ironic thing is that the atheist who reasons in this way is already well enroute to becoming a believer in endorsing that first premise. For if he is a normal and decent human being, he cannot but regard evil as just that, something that is truly evil—and thereby something whose absence is much to be wished for. And so over and above the preceding syllogism he becomes committed to the following line of reasoning:

- Only if the world were the creation of a benevolent God would it contain no evil.

- A world without evil is greatly to be desired.

Therefore: The existence of a benevolent God is greatly to be desired.

But as the Judeo-Christian tradition sees it it is the yearning for the Lord that is the crux of faith.[2] And so the atheist who invokes the Problem of Evil as a core argument for his position is already well enroute to theism in the Judeo-Christian tradition.

In sum, the Problem of Evil simply is not a weapon made ready-to-hand for the purposes of the atheist. For it to have telling effect—indeed even to depict the world's evil as a real problem—presupposes a commitment on the exponent's part to the idea that a benevolent formative force should by rights be at work in the operations of the world.

In reality, the dialectical position of the atheist who invokes the Problem of Evil argues against the opponent's position via premises that the addressee accepts but the arguer himself does not. And this is not demonstrative but rather the very quintessence of a merely *ad hominen* argument. The atheist can indeed deploy such an argument as a provocation in order to issue a challenge. The atheist can invoke the problem to make the point that the theist has work to do. But when he sets out to use it unconditionally and categorically to argue for his own position, he is treading on very problematic ground.

NOTES FOR CHAPTER 9

[1]   As Leibniz noted in his *Theodicy: malum causa habet non efficientem sed deficientem.* G. W. Leibnioz, *Thodicy*, VI 115 and VI 122.

[2]   "Faith is the substance of things hoped for" (Hebrews 11:1). "To believe in God is to yearn for his existence" wrote Miguel de Unamuno in his 1913 classic, *The Tragic Sense of Life*.

Chapter 10

RATIONALITY, SELF-INTEREST, ALTRUISM, AND OBLIGATION

As a principle of practice, the doctrine of self-interest pivots on the idea that the only considerations providing a cogent reason for an agent's actions are those which relate to the individual's own best interests. The sole appropriate reason for acting is matters of "looking out for No. 1". Thus to be rational is to be selfish.

At first view this sort of view looks pretty nasty in its self-centered orientation. Is this really the sort of person we would want to have as children, friends, and relatives. But the matter is actually more subtle than it seems to be on first view. For the issue clearly pivots on just what it is that is in an individual's best interests.

There is a crucial difference between self-interest and selfishness exactly because self-interest can—and should—encompass the interest of others.

The reality of it is that there are going to be three major alternatives here:

- *Crude self-interest.* An individual's interest encompasses only that which is at stake with his own "material" welfare (preeminently health, living standard, and personal consumptions).

- *Narrowly enlightened self-interest.* An individual's self-interest encompasses not only his own well-being, but also that of others in whom he *takes an interest* (such as relations, friends, neighbors, colleagues, etc.).

- *Broadly enlightened self-interest.* An individual's self-interest encompasses not only his own well-being, but also that of the others in whom he *has* (that is, *ought to take*) and interest—something which ultimately encompasses all of his fellows (and perhaps even developed creatures at large)—presumably in line with their proximity.

That is to say, enlightened self-interest will always make a significant degree of interiorization of the interests of others.

One significant point immediately emerges from this view of the situation: There is nothing inappropriate or improper to a policy of action on the basis of self-interest once that self-interest comes to be construed in a sufficiently enlightened way. As a matter of fact, as one moves in this direction the boundary between self-interest and altruism gradually vanishes. Even the most generous-minded of moralist can no longer object to a commitment to self-interest once that interest is so understood as to encompass a commitment to the interests of others—as indeed it ought.

But that of course is not how traditional self-interest exponents have understood the matter. Throughout they have insisted on a rather crude and blundered rather than a broad and generous construal of self-interest.

But is such enlightenment rational? David Hume has been their most prominent philosophical spokesman here. Hume contended that there is no *rational* basis for preferring massive benefit to others over a trivial benefit to self. He wrote: "It is not contrary to reason to preface the destruction of the whole world to prefer the destruction of the whole world to the scratching of my finger."[1]

To assess this position rightly, we must go back to basics and ask: "What is it that makes something rationally preferable at all?" And here the appropriate response is:

> X is rationally preferable to Y if (other thing equal) an X-instantiating item is better than a Y-instantiating one.

For to all sensible intents and purposes we have the chain of equations: "preferable to" = "better than" = "deserves to be chosen" = "would be chosen by a rational agent."

Given this view of rational preferability, Hume's position is undermined by the following course of reasoning:

1. Rational people will seek to satisfy their *needs*.

2. We have a need for a congenial (approbation-worthy) environment as a life-setting

3. Only a human environment where people care for others (i.e., are at least somewhat altruistic) is congenial to humans as actually constituted and thereby worthy of approbation by them.

4. The welfare and well being of others—properly understood—is thus something that actually forms part of our own needs.

5. Only such a society—one whose people are enlightened with respect of self-interest—would be preferable (other things equal).

As it moves from the narrowly concerned to enlightened self-interest the transit along these views in effect moves preferability from selfishness to altruism.

But what is it that speaks for this? Why should this transit be seen as proper and appropriate?

The answer is straightforward. It is our rationality that urges this step. And here Hume is simply wrong.

What reason demands of a rational being is using its rationality to exploit its opportunities for the realization of "the good". And here the good must be comprehensively construed to encompass not only what is to the immediate period advantage the agent but also that which he takes—or qua rational being *should* take—an interest.

But why take an interest in the well-being of others? The answer is straightforward. Because I am a rational being.

Here too a rather straightforward line of thought is at work.

1. Any being on a point of view itself as a rational being should—not to its own advantage must—actually regard itself as such.

2. Any being that regards itself as a natural being should prize and value that rationality. (For such a being there is little that would be more logic than "to loose its reason.")

3. Any rational being that prizes its own reason will, qua rational, do so because it sees reason as validity.

4. But if reason is indeed instructive, it is so in general wherever we may find it.

5. In consequence, a rational being will value reason not just in itself but in all rational beings. That is he will view all rational beings as bearers of value.

6. But that which has value deserves to be rational, by anyone capable of valuing things—oneself included.

7. Therefore a rational being will, by virtue of that rationality, also value other rational beings, and accordingly cannot be indifferent to and mindful of their well being.

8. Accordingly a rational being will (to some degree) rationalize the well being of others and will (to some degree) see this as being a part of its own best interest.

As this line of thought indicates, the recommendations of rationality itself demand that for rational beings there is a natural impetus to the enlightenment of self-interest and correspondingly a rational transit from self-interest to altruism.

Of course, it must and can be acknowledged that there are differences in regard to the self-interest of others. Clearly people do not stand on a plane of equality in the extent to which their interest is appropriately encompassed in the interests of others. It is only to be expected that a husband should care for the interests of his wife, a mother for those of her child, a friend for those of his friends. But to some small extent, at least, the interest of others—even strangers—form part of our own. (And arguably this could even be maintained with respect to animals.)

Certain obligations to others are incurred voluntarily—they become incumbent upon one in virtue of roles one voluntarily chooses to undertake—ad physicians, sea captains, husbands, or fathers. Other obligations become incumbent upon are by virtue of what one *is* rather than by virtue of what one does. These are the obligations that are mandated upon us in virtue of being a human being, a native born American, or a child of particular parents. The obligations that we have as rational beings are of this automatic rather than elective variety.

A cardinal obligation that is encountered in every rational agent is that of exerting effort for the realization of the good—of so acting that the world is—at least to some extent a better place for one's presence in it. Even rather narrowly construed self-interest demands that one avails oneself of at least some opportunities for an enhancement of the good and a diminution of the bad.

Self-improvement in the sense of making oneself a better person is a rational mandate for beings situated as we in fact are. Minimally this calls for becoming a decent human being, a "Mensch" is a moral requisite. And maximally—at the level of supererogation—it calls for being a moral exemplar, a saint. But that of course is something else again. Performing works of supererogation is undoubtedly praiseworthy, but it is not obligatory. Obligations merely set a minimum standard for ethical worth. It is clearly possible that people can go beyond this and laudable when they do so. But this involves going beyond what morality demands of us. It can demand that we be good people, but not that we become saints. This is a demand one can only impose on oneself. As such it is not irrational but arational—something that transcends the reach of reason. But here Hume was only half right. He tied morality to interest, which is right enough. But he did not do justice to the fact that interest extends beyond the crude and selfish into the realm of the enlightened. In this regard it is ironic to see him as a thinker of the "Enlightenment".

NOTES FOR CHAPTER 10

[1] David Hume, *A Treatise of Human Nature*, Bk. II., pt. 3, sect. 3.

Chapter 11

WHAT IS PRAGMATISM?

Pragmatism is an approach to philosophical issues predicated on the idea that practice is the paramount arbiter in our affairs—even in matters of theory. The root conception goes back to the doctrines of the Academic Sceptics of classical antiquity who despaired of achieving certain knowledge (*epistêmê*) and looked to plausibility (*to pithanon*), regarding efficacy in matters of practice as affording our best available guide here.[1] It was, however, Immanuel Kant who introduced the term "pragmatic" into philosophy, saying that a principle is *pragmatic* (rather than *moral*) when it is "a principle regarding the means to a specific end [which need not be specifically moral]."[2]

As matters evolved, with the renaissance of pragmatism in the American School of Pierce, James, and Dewey, pragmatism became many things to many people. In his classic 1908 paper on "The Thirteen Pragmatisms"[3] A. O. Lovejoy characterized them as follows:

1 and 2. A semiotic pragmatism holding that the *meaning* of propositions pivots on future consequences. This divides into two parts: (1) consequences to be anticipated if the proposition is true, and (2) consequences to be anticipated if people accept the proposition.

3. An epistemic pragmatism holding that the *verification* or substantiation of a proposition pivots on the realization of the future expectations that they authorize.

4. The semantical thesis that propositions are not true or false timelessly but eventually acquire truth or falsity according as their inherent predictions in due course "work out" in the sense of being realized or disconfined.

5. The cognate semantical thesis that results when "working out" is construed not predictively as being borne out by events, but rather as proving useful (productive) in applicative practice.

6. The metaphysical doctrine that the future is "open" in the sense that the truth or falsity of claims about it is not, as yet, determined in a definite

way. (Proportions about the future thus are, or can be, devoid of a truth status.)

7. The psychological thesis that people's acceptance of the truth of propositions pivots on their providing "the maximal combination of satisfactions".

8. The epistemic doctrine that the truth of a proposition is to be assessed in terms of its "satisfyingness" in a way that transcends the specifically cognitive satisfactions to conclude any sort of satisfaction elsewhere.

9. This is tantamount to 8 with the "satisfyingness" at issue taken to include the specifically *cognitive* satisfactions (in ways that transcend the purely predictive concerns of 3).

10. This is the thesis that "axioms are postulates"—that truth can be *made* (rather than discovered) and that this making can be validated as practical need—i.e., the satisfaction of our human *requirements*.

11. The psychological doctrine that our human mental faculties and processes have so evolved that assent to certain propositions—such as "pain is bad"—is (not merely useful but) effectively unavoidable for us.

12. The stance of maintaining the legitimacy (and indeed co-equal legitimacy) of assenting to those propositions which are needed (1) to make intelligible sense of our experience, (2) to facilitate our moral commitments, and (3) to satisfy our emotional needs and esthetic inclinations.

13. The meaning-as-function idea of the semiotic primacy of purpose inherent in the circumstance that every concept, idea, belief, or proposition comes to be what it is because of the purpose it serves—i.e., through its relation to our ends and plans of action.

Upon surveying this ground, Lovejoy proceeded to reclassify his thirteen pragmatisms into four groups, essentially as follows:

I. *Semiotic (Meaning-Determinative) Pragmatism*: Pragmatic theories of meaning

—Numbers 1, 2, 13

II. *Semantical (Truth-Determinative) Pragmatism*: A pragmatic theory about the nature (or definition) of truth

—Number 3

III. *Epistemological Pragmatism*: Pragmatic theories about the criteriology of truth (or tests of the validity of judgment)

—Numbers 4, 5, 7, 8, 9, 10, 11, 12

IV. *Metaphysical Pragmatism*: Pragmatism as an ontological theory about the nature of reality

—Number 6

Lovejoy accordingly saw pragmatism as a mélange of different (and in some instances rival) contentions.[4] And he regarded this state of affairs as virtually fatal to pragmatism's claims as a meaningful philosophical position.

But this view of the matter is very questionable. For pragmatism is in fact a theoretical stance of a general orientation rather than a single definite doctrine—a line of approach which can be developed along rather different lines. Its inherent generality clearly does not constitute a valid objection, but is simply an indication that, like other philosophical positions (idealism, empiricism, materialism), pragmatism can be elaborated in different directions. Pragmatism's prismatically many-sided nature means that the prime question for philosophical deliberation is not "Is pragmatism plausible?" but rather "Can really plausible versions of pragmatism be articulated?"

Admittedly, any attempt to articulate *the* uniquely correct version of pragmatism is destined to add simply another item to the long list. Accepting this situation as effectively inevitable, the present discussion of the problem "What is Pragmatism?" sets itself a modest and limited goal. All that it will endeavor to do is to propose an answer to this question which is hermeneutically clear, substantively cogent, and in general conformity with the "spirit"—the aims and aspirations—which prevail throughout the endeavor to articulate a pragmatic philosophy.

It is clear on this basis that two salient ideas provide the basis of the present exposition of pragmatism. They are

- the fundamental and formative role of the conception of practice, function, and purposive endeavor.

- the governing and controlling force of the factor of purposive efficacy and factual effectiveness.

The two formatively characteristic issues for a pragmatic approach are inherent in the question (1) What is the aim of the enterprise—what is the characteristic objective at issue? And (2) How efficient and effective is the idea under consideration in serving their purpose and accepting this function? And so, what the pragmatists accordingly asks from the very outset is: How effective is the item at issue at accomplishing its intended work?

Pragmatism, so conceived, is a fundamentally normative theory whose yardstick of appropriateness is afforded by functional efficacy. Effective and efficient goal attainment in pragmatism's standard of merit within the particular context at issue. Pragmatism's imperative is: "Evaluative adequacy in terms of functional efficacy." Indeed, given that theorizing—of any sort—always proceeds in the setting of correlative aims and purposes, pragmatism takes the line that theorizing is itself a praxis whose effectiveness in goal attainment is the key to adequacy. On this basis pragmatism see praxis as the arbiter of theory: the assessment of adequacy is guided in the arbitrament of practice.

So regarded, pragmatism invokes two further salient considerations:

- That anything of the nature of an instrumentality—any sort of tool, method, modus operandi, and the like—calls for being assessed in terms of functional adequacy, that is, in terms of its capacity effectively and facilitation the realization of its correlative purpose, and

- That concepts, ideas, beliefs have a functional dimension—except for the sake of clarification, explanation communication and the like—and thereby ultimately for the guidance of action. That they are tools, instrumentalities and methodological resources, whose validity can therefore be assessed in terms of functional adequacy.

And so, while Lovejoy was quite right in indicating that different sorts of issues are at stake here, he did pragmatic less than justice in failing to see that all of them are simply so many applications and instrumentations of one single basic idea, to wit:

It is the mode of functioning (the modus operandi) of any given sort of thing that is prompted for defining it as the sort of thing it is, and insofar as any purposes are at issue with this mode of functioning the evaluation of appropriateness will hinge in consideration of functional efficacy.

It would accordingly be a grave error to interpret the considerations adduced by Lovejoy as constituting a valid criticism—let alone refutation—of pragmatism. The lesson is simply that here, as elsewhere, a philosopher should be specific about the views he intends to propose or discuss. And the ultimate test of a many-sided and internally diversified doctrine like pragmatism is surely not that of the question "Are there some version of pragmatism that is in some way deficit and unacceptable?" but rather that of the opposite question "Is there some versions of pragmatism, broadly construed, that are in their own way adequate and acceptable?" And it is this approach to the issue that will constitute our guiding principle here.

Viewed in this light, it should become clear that two pivotal pragmatic theses are going to be at issue:

- Theses and contentions are true when they guide practice with maximal efficacy.

- The touchstone of truth and reality is operational efficacy: To be is to act and in the final analysis a thing is what it does, its nature constituted by the way it acts upon and interacts with others.

On this basis, the tenor of pragmatism can be illustrated by these classically central concepts of philosophy: the true, the good, and the beautiful.

Illustration No 1: The Issue of Truth

In dealing with truth and falsity, philosophers have traditionally set out from the question: What is the nature of truth? Just what are we saying when we characterize a claim or contention as true or false? A pragmatist, by contrast, will begin by asking: What is the purpose and function of the distinction between truth and falsity. Just what is at stake in distinguishing the true from the false? Just what is it that we are trying to achieve when we characterize some claim or contention as true? What purpose is it we have in view in the enterprise of rational inquiry within whose aegis we seek to implement the distinction between the true and the false? What is it that we propose to do with the claims we class as true?

And the answer here is pretty straightforward. We propose to use true claims in two ways. First, in *theoretical* applications to answer our questions, organize our knowledge, structure our views about how matters stand in the realm of fact. And second in *practical* applications to implement our beliefs in order to guide our actions and to canalize our behavior. The function of implementing the true/false distinction is, to achieve a workable understanding of how matters stand in the real of fact, and coordinatively to guide our actions adequately in matters of action—in sum, to achieve both theoretical and practical satisfaction.

For the pragmatists then, the crux of employing and implementing the true/false distinction lies in the aims for which this distinction is instituted. And on this basis, truth is what truth does.

Illustration No. 2: The Issue of Right

In dealing with right and wrong, philosophers have traditionally set out from the question: What is the nature of right? Just what are we saying when we characterize a person's act as right or wrong? A pragmatist by contrast, will begin by asking: Why is it that moral codes for distinguishing right from wrong are instantiated in human communities? What purposes are realized by distinguishing right from wrong? And the answer here is, pretty straightforward: to canalize people's behavior into communally benign channels; to get people to behave in ways that serve the best interests of the community at large; to get individuals to behave in ways that guide their interactions with others into patterns that best serve the interests of all concerned—in sum, to domesticate people into being effective members of a generally benign community.

Illustration No. 3: The Issue of Beauty

Again, in dealing with aesthetics, philosophers have traditionally asked: What is the nature of beauty? A pragmatist, by contrast, will begin by asking: what are the purposes achieved by instituting the distinctions between the beautiful and the ugly? Just what is it are to do about it when we characterize some item as beautiful?

And the answer here proceeds in relation to the matter of appreciation— of enjoyment and encouragement, of providing for enlightenment and insight, of enlarging horizons and expanding sympathies, and enabling others to participate in such reactions. Beauty in act and nature is valued not just for its own sake but because people are able to enter into its enjoyment and appreciation as a basis for experiences that conduce to the enrichment of life.

* * *

In each case, the matter of the appropriate use of the distinctions at issue (true/false, right/wrong, beautiful/ugly) is addressed and resolved with reference to the aims and purposed for which the distinction is instituted as an instrumentality of consideration and communication.

As all these cases illustrate, pragmatism's basic idea is that an understanding of such philosophically fundamental distinctions as true/false, right/wrong, beautiful/ugly is best achieved by looking at these matters in a functionalistic perspective, approaching the issue from the aegis of the question of the purposes served by operating with the conceptions at issue. The fundamental idea is that the terms and ideas at issue are instrumentalities, conceptual tools for achieving certain purposes. And—so pragmatism has it—it is by looking to the area and purpose at issue with our conceptual instrumentalities that the nature of what is at issue is best and most clearly comes to light.

Put a different perspective to those many different "versions of pragmatism" about which critics since A. O. Lovejoy have been wont to complain. For in the light of the present deliberations those different positions are not different pragmatisms at all, but merely different application or employments of one single unified pragmatic idea—viz. that of a single mode of quality control over our proceedings in very different areas of discussion—one that proceeds in terms of functional efficacy with respect to the aims and purposes characteristic of the particular domain at issue. Pragmatism is thus an approach to philosophical explanation and understanding effectively based on the spirit of the biblical dictum: "By their fruits shall ye know them."

NOTES FOR CHAPTER 11

[1] The historical issues are canvassed in the author's *Scepticism* (Oxford: Basil Blackwell, 1980).

NOTES FOR CHAPTER 11

[2] "Eternal Peace," sect. 2.

[3] A. O. Lovejoy, "The Thirteen Pragmatisms," *The Journal of Philosophy and Scientific Methods,* vol. 5 (1908), pp. 5-39; reprinted in his *The Thirteen Pragmatisms and Other Essays* (Baltimore: Johns Hopkins Press, 1963; rptd. 1983).

[4] The subsequent emergence of social pragmatism made matters still worse in this regard.

Chapter 12

THE TRANSFORMATION OF AMERICAN PHILOSOPHY

1. DISCIPLINARY GROWTH

The motive force of the contemporary transformation of American philosophy is manpower. For perhaps the most striking feature of professional philosophy in North America at this historic juncture is the scope and scale of its personnel roster. The discipline presently has more than 8,000 members, and the comprehensive *Directory of American Philosophers* for 2004-05 lists some 14,000 philosophers affiliated to colleges and universities in the USA and Canada, while in the late 1930s, on the eve of World War II, the membership of the American Philosophical Association stood at some 750. And at that time there were some 20 philosophical societies organized on a topical or regional basis while by 2000 there were some 150 of them.[1] This explosion in the scale of the enterprise has had a substantial array of portentous consequences.

The first and most obvious of these is an enormous growth in the literature of the subject. With the "publish or perish" syndrome at work in higher education, an increase in the volume of publication has kept pace with the growth of the philosophical community. For the fact is that American philosophers are quite productive. They publish well over 3,000 books per annum nowadays. And issue by issue they fill up the pages of over 175 journals.[2] Given that some 7,000 philosophical publications (books, monographs, or articles) appear annually in North America, and a roughly similar number of papers for symposia and conferences, there is simply no practicable way for anyone to "keep up with the field".

The size and scope of the academic establishment exerts a crucial formative influence on the nature of contemporary American philosophy. The increase in people and publications has so worked out as to effect a transformation in the discipline of philosophy itself by perfectly natural and readily understandable general mechanisms.

2. SPECIALIZATION, DIVISION OF LABOR, TECHNICALIZATION

Since there are only so many hours in a day, there is only so much that a given individual can fit into their cognitive warehouse of thought and attention. But the domain of science and scholarship has been growing exponentially with ever new materials emerging in ever new categories. The inevitable result is the ongoing selectivity of specialization and division of labor.

Accordingly the individual's unavoidable response is to have an increasingly contracting focus on matters of detail. The only alternative open here is ongoingly to narrow the range of one's concerns. Deliberations become ever more tightly concentrated, more narrowly targeted on microspecifics and increasingly given to an ever more elaborate scrutiny of subtle differences and details. And so it becomes ever more difficult to see the forest for the trees, to keep the big picture in view. The field becomes increasingly specialized and technical with its inquiries disintegrating into a proliferation of cottage industries. The overall situation becomes one of specialists talking to other specialists.

And just this is what has been happening in philosophy. American philosophers nowadays by and large see themselves, accurately enough, as cultivating one academic specialty among many others—as technicians laboring at some specialty within the realm of ideas.

There is a certain irony in the entry of substantial specialization into the practice of philosophy. For by its very nature it is philosophy's task to provide "the big picture" and to address "the big questions" about reality and man's place within it. And this calls for generalism—for forming a synoptic view across a broad range of issues. Insofar as the present-day dynamics inherent in the practice of philosophizing makes for specialization and division of labor, it countervails against the versatility illustrated by Aristotle, Descartes, Leibniz, Kant, et. al. In an era of limited expertise in specialized domains, the label "polymathic" is virtually one of derogation. And yet it is exactly this that is called for by being a *philosopher* rather than merely an ethicist, a logician, or an historian of philosophical ideas.

All the same, the prominence of specialization gives a more professional and technical cast to contemporary American philosophizing in comparison to that of other times and places. Historians of philosophy are nowadays increasingly preoccupied with matters of small-scale philosophical and conceptual microdetail. And philosophical investigations make increasingly extensive use of the formal machinery of semantics, modal logic, compilation theory, learning theory, etc. Ever heavier theoretical armaments are brought to bear on ever smaller problem-targets in ways that journal readers will occasionally wonder whether the important principle that technicalities should never be multiplied beyond necessity have been lost sight of.

3. AGENDA ENLARGEMENT AND DISCIPLINE FRAGMENTATION

As more people crowd into a field of investigation with fixed topical boundaries (as in natural science) there will only be room for them by raising the level of the domain by means of more powerful technology—one has to erect skyscrapers as it were. But a field with moveable boundaries (such as philosophy, mathematics, and the human sciences) the field can expand outwards into virgin territory that has not previously been explored and settled. And the fact that those many hundreds of philosophers are looking for something to do that is not simply a matter of re-exploring familiar ground has created a substantial population pressure for more philosophical Lebensraum. New subfields and new problem-areas spring forth.

The rapid growth of "applied philosophy"—that is, philosophical reflection about detailed issues in science, law, business, social affairs, computer use, and the like—is a striking structural feature of contemporary North American philosophy. In particular, the past three decades have seen a great proliferation of narrowly focused philosophical investigations of particular issues in areas such as economic justice, social welfare, ecology, abortion, population policy, military defense, and so on. This situation illustrates the most characteristic feature of contemporary English-language philosophizing: the emphasis on detailed investigation of special issues and themes. For better or for worse, Anglophone philosophers have in recent years tended to stay away from large-scale abstract matters of wide and comprehensive scope, characteristic of the earlier era of Whitehead or Dewey, and nowadays incline to focus their investigations on issues of greater detail that relate to and grow out of those larger issues of traditional concern.

Agenda-enlargement is accordingly one of the most striking features of contemporary American philosophy. The pages of its journals and the programs of its meetings bristle with discussions of issues that would seem bizarre to their predecessors of earlier days and to present-day philosophers of other places. For example, one recent program of the annual meeting of the Eastern Division of American Philosophical Association included papers on "Is it Dangerous to Demystify Human Rights?", "Difference and the Differend in Derrida and Lyotard", "Animal Rights Theory and the Diminishment of Infants", "On the Ecological Consequences of Alphabetical Literacy", "Is Polygamy Good Feminism?", "The Ethics of the Free Market", "Planetary Projection of the Multiple Self on Films", "The Moral Collapse of the University", and "The Construction of Female Political Identity."[3] Entire philosophical societies are dedicated to the pursuit of issues now deemed philosophical that no-one would have dreamt of considering so a generation ago. (Some examples are the societies for Machines and Mentality, for Informal Logic and Critical Thinking, for the Study of Ethics and Animals, for Philosophy and Literature, for Analytical Feminism, and for Philosophy of Sex and Love.) The turning of philosophy from globally general, large-scale issues to more narrowly focused investigations of matters of microscopically fine-grained detail is a characteristic feature of American philosophy after World War II. Its flourishing use of the case-study method in philosophy is a striking phenomenon for which no one philosopher can claim credit—to a contemporary observer it seems like the pervasively spontaneous expression of "the spirit of the times".

The inevitable result of this agenda enlargement has been a revolutionizing of the structure of philosophy itself by way of taxonomic complexification. The present-day picture of the taxonomic lay of the land in North America philosophy is thus vastly more complex and ramified than anything that has preceded it. The taxonomy of the subject has burst for good and all the bounds of the ancient tripartite scheme of logic, metaphysics and ethics. Specialization and division of labor runs rampant, and cottage industries are the order of the day. The situation has grown so complex and diversified that one English-language encyclopedia of philosophy[4] cautiously abstains from providing any taxonomy of philosophy whatsoever. (This phenomenon also goes a long way towards explaining why no one has written a comprehensive history of philosophy that carries through to the present-day scene.[5]) Philosophy—which ought by mission and tradition to be an integration of knowledge—has itself become increasingly disintegrated. The growth of the discipline has forced it beyond the limits of feasible surveillance by a single mind. After World War II it becomes literally impossible for American philosophers to keep up with what their colleagues were writing.

And so one striking aspect of contemporary American philosophy is its fragmentation. The scale and complexity of the enterprise is such that if one seeks in contemporary American philosophy for a consensus on the problem agenda, let alone for agreement on the substantive issues, then one is predestined to look in vain. Here theory diversity and doctrinal dissonance are the order of the day. Such unity as American philosophy affords is that of an academic industry, not that of a single doctrinal orientation or school. Every doctrine, every theory, every approach finds its devotees somewhere within the overall community.[6] On most of the larger issues there are no significant majorities. To be sure, some uniformities are apparent at the localized level. (In the San Francisco Bay area one's philosophical discussions might well draw on model theory, in Princeton possible worlds would be bought in, in Pittsburgh, pragmatic themes would be prominent, and so on.) But in matters of method and doctrine there is a proliferation of schools and tendencies, and there are no all-pervasively dominant trends. Balkanization reigns supreme.

4. INACCESSIBILITY

The prominence of specialization gives a far more professional and technical cast to contemporary American philosophizing in comparison to that of other times and places. Philosophers nowadays generally write for an audience of their fellow academics and have little interest in (or prospect of) addressing a wider public of intelligent readers at large. There can be little doubt that the increasing technicalization of philosophy has been achieved at the expense of its wider accessibility—and indeed even to its accessibility to members of the profession.

Its increasing specialization has impelled philosophy towards the ivory tower. And so, the most recent years have accordingly seen something of a fall from grace of philosophy in American culture—not that there was ever all that much grace to fall from. For many years, the *Encyclopedia Britannica* published an annual supplement entitled *19XY Book of the Year*, dealing with the events of the previous year under such rubrics as World Politics, Health, Music, etc. Until the 1977 volume's coverage of the preceding year's developments, a section of philosophy was always included in this annual series. But thereafter, philosophy vanished—without so much as a word of explanation. Seemingly the year of America's bicentennial saw the disappearance of philosophy from the domain of things that interest Americans. At approximately the same time, *Who's Who in America* drastically curtailed its coverage of philosophers (and academics generally). And during this same time period, various vehicles of public opinion—

ranging from *Time Magazine* to *The New York Times*—voiced laments over the irrelevance of recent philosophy to the problems of the human condition and the narcissistic absorption of philosophers in logical and linguistic technicalities that rendered the discipline irrelevant to the problems and interests of nonspecialists.[7]

It is remarkable that this popular alienation from philosophy's ivory-towerishness came at just the time when philosophers in the U.S.A. were beginning to return to problems on the agenda of public policy and personal concern. The flowering of applied ethics (medical ethics, business ethics, environmental ethics, and the like), of virtue ethics (trust, hope, neighborliness, etc.), of social ethics (distributive justice, privacy, individual rights, etc.) and of such philosophical hyphenations as philosophy-and-society—and even philosophy-and-agriculture!—can also be dated from just this period. By one of those ironies not uncommon in the pages of history, philosophy returned to the issues of the day at virtually the very moment when the wider public gave up thinking of the discipline as relevant to its concerns. (To be sure, this occurred at a technical level at which "the general reader" may no feel altogether comfortable.)

The fact is that philosophy has little or no place in America *popular* (as opposed to *academic*) culture, since at this level people's impetus to global understanding is accommodated—in America, at least—by religion rather than philosophy. Philosophical issues are by nature complicated, and Americans do not relish complications and have a marked preference for answers over questions. The nature of the case is such that philosophers must resort to careful distinctions and saving qualifications. And in this regard Americans do not want to know where the complexities lurk but yearn for the proverbial one-armed experts who do not constantly say "on the other hand". Technical philosophy leaves "the man in the street" cold. We are a practical people who want efficient solutions (as witness the vast market for self-help books with their dogmatic nostrums).

However, while philosophy nowadays makes virtually no impact on the wider culture of North America, its place in higher education is secure. To be sure, of all undergraduates in American colleges and universities, only about half of one percent *major* in Philosophy (compared with nearly three percent for English and over fifteen percent for Business and Management).[8] But owing to philosophy's role in meeting "distribution requirements" it has secured a prominent place in the curricula of post-secondary education. Unlike the United Kingdom, where post-World War II philosophers adopted a very technical and narrowly conceived idea of what the job of philosophy is—with the result of effectively assuring the discipline's declining role in the educational system—in America philosophy has managed not only to survive but to thrive in higher education. It has done so in large measure by taking a practicalist and accommodationist turn. American philosophers have been very flexible in bending with the wind. When society demanded "relevancy to social concerns", a new specialty of "applied philosophers" sprang forth to provide it. When problems of medical ethics or of feminist perspectivism occupy the society, a bevy of eager young philosophers stands ready to leap into the breach.

5. ATTENTION DIFFUSION AND THE FADING OF "THE GREAT MAN" THEORY

With the exponential increase in the number of academic philosophers at large there also occurs an exponential increase in

- the number of philosophers who publish two or more papers;

- the number of philosophers who publish books;

- the number of philosophers whose publications are intensively considered by a particular fraction of the overall community.

But as one moves down this list *rate* at which this exponential increase occurs becomes less and less.[9]

Accordingly, consider the fraction

$$\frac{volume\ of\ literature\ devoted\ to\ the\ work\ of\ a\ given\ philosopher}{volume\ of\ the\ literature\ at\ large}$$

This might be called the *attention-ratio* of the work of a given philosopher. And the reality of it is that in a situation of exponential growth the general tendency is for this ratio to diminish steadily.

With an exponential membership expansion of any scientific or scholarly field there will be less attention devoted to the work (however good) of any given individual. The situation is depicted schematically in Display 1. And might be characterized as the *diffusion of attention*. In such a situation of experiential growth it transpires that however important a given individual may be in comparison to others in relation to the community as a whole has stature will shrink.

Even the most influential of contemporary American philosophers is simply yet another—somewhat larger—fish in a very populous sea. The extent to which professionally solid and significant work is currently produced by academics outside the high-visibility limelight is not sufficiently recognized. The smaller fish play an increasingly prominent role simply because there are so many more of them.[10]

Display 1

Number (N) of scholars	Number of scholars citing the work of a given (important) individuals	(n/N) × 100
100	50	50%
1,000	400	40%
10,000	3,200	30%
100,000	25,000	20%

NOTE: The figures are illustrative only, intended to suggest that the ratio $n \div N$ decreases linearly as N increases exponentially.

In the past, the philosophical situation of academically developed countries could be described by indicating a few giants whose work towered over the philosophical landscape like a great mountain range, and whose issues and discussions defined the agenda of the philosophizing of their place and time. Once upon a time, the philosophical stage was dominated by a small handful of greats. Consider German philosophy in the 19th century, for example. Here the philosophical scene, like the country itself, was an aggregate of principalities—presided over by such ruling figures as Kant, Fichte, Hegel, Schelling, Schopenhauer, and a score of other philosophical princelings. But in North America, this "heroic age" of philosophy is now a thing of the past.

In the philosophical environment of the past, the role of the great figures was more prominent, and the writings of philosophers established a balance of indebtedness to "big names" as against "modest contributors" that tilted much more in the direction of the "big names". For better or for worse, we have entered into a new philosophical era where what counts is not just a dominant elite but a vast host of lesser mortals. Principalities are thus notable in their absence, and the scene is more like that of medieval Europe—a collection of baronies. Scattered here and there in separated castles, a prominent individual gains a local following of loyal friends or enemies. But no one among the academic philosophers of today manages to impose their agenda on more than a minimal fraction of the larger, internally diversified community.

Until around 1914, it was religion that exerted the dominant influence on American philosophers. During the 1914-1960 era natural science served as the prime source of inspiration. But over the past generation the sources of inspiration have become greatly diversified. The fact is that at present philosophy is a garden where 100 flowers bloom. In recent years the source of influence has fragmented across the whole academic board. Some look for inspiration to psychology (especially to Freud), others to economics (from Marx to von Neumann), yet others to literature, or to law, or to ... The list goes on and on. Contemporary American philosophy does not have the form of a histogram with a few major trends; it is a complex mosaic of many different and competing approaches.

And so the Great Man Theory no longer holds; a faithful picture of the work of the entire community simply cannot be conveyed by considering the work of its three (or ten or hundred) greatest members. The only way to give an accurate account of the community as a whole in its present configuration is to proceed not personalistically via individuals but holistically via statistics. An account in terms of representative Great Men no longer works. Of course there will indeed still be giants but their role in the overall scheme of things is increasingly diminished. Strange though it may sound, the role of important individuals (so considered in the relation of others) becomes of ongoingly diminished importance in the overall scheme of things. As the points grow the big fish play an increasingly diminished role. The three (or ten or hundred) biggest of them constitute an increasingly diminished part of the pond as a whole.

The fact is that those bigger fish do not typify what the sea as a whole has to offer. Matters of philosophical history aside, some of the salient themes and issues with which American philosophers are grappling at the present time are

- applied ethics: ethical issues in the professions (medicine, business, law, etc.);

- computer issues: artificial intelligence, "can machines think?", the epistemology of information processing;

- rationality and its ramifications;

- social implications of medical technology (abortion, euthanasia, right to life, medical research issues, informed consent);

- feminist issues;

- social and economic justice, distributive policies, equality of opportunity, human rights;

- truth and meaning in mathematics and formalized languages;

- the merits and demerits of scepticism and relativism regarding knowledge and morality;

- the nature of personhood and the rights and obligations of persons.

None of these issues were put on the problem-agenda of present concern by any one particular philosopher. None arose out of a preoccupation with fundamental aspects of some already well-established issue. None arose out of one particular philosophical text or discussion. They blossomed forth like the leaves of a tree in springtime appearing in various places at once under the formative impetus of the Zeitgeist of societal concern. The nature of American philosophy today is such that for the most part new ideas and tendencies have come to prominence not because of the influential impact of some specific contribution or worker but because of the disaggregated effects of a host of writers working across a wide frontier of individual efforts. In many and indeed perhaps most instance the principal recent innovations in philosophy—its salient programs and projects—can no longer be identified with the inaugurating individual of any of the contributing "greats". Philosophical innovation today is generally not the response to the preponderant effort of pace-setting individuals but a genuinely collective effort that is best characterized in statistical terms.

6. DEMOCRATIZATION

The descriptive account of a field of intellectual endeavor confronts two key questions:

1. What is the state of the discipline as a whole? What ideas and innovations are astir?

2. What are the contributions of its leading practitioners? What has its top elite been contributing to the field?

In philosophy these two issues have traditionally been conjoined in a way that enables the response to question (1) be developed by way of responding to questions (2). This is, in effect, the classic model of philosophical historiography. But it is the characteristic argument of the current transformation of American philosophy that this is no longer the case. The experience of the discipline has had the result the addressing the question (2) regarding its key problems is no longer an adequate approach to handling question (1) regarding the state of the discipline as a whole. The traditional Great Man Theory of historiography is no longer available in relation to American Philosophy.

It is the salient thesis of this discussion that this Classical model of intellectual Historiography no longer applies to American Philosophy in its contemporary configuration. The discipline has expanded to a point where its scope and diversity is such that an example of the work of its leading practitioners is no longer able to give a faithful picture of the development of the whole.

A century ago, the historian Henry Adams deplored the end of the predominance of the great and the good in American politics and the emergence of a new order based on the dominance of masses and their often self-appointed representatives. Control of the political affairs of the nation was flowing from the hands of a cultural elite into that of the unimposing, albeit vociferous, spokesmen for the faceless masses. In short, democracy was setting in. Exactly this same transformation from the preeminence of great figures to the predominance of mass movements is now, one hundred years on, the established situation in even so intellectual an enterprise as philosophy. In its present configuration, American philosophy indicates that the "revolt of the masses", which Ortega y Gasset thought characteristic of our era, manifests itself not only in politics and social affairs but in intellectual culture also and even in philosophy.[11] A cynic might character-ize the current situation as a victory of the troglodytes over the giants.[12] The condition of American philosophy today is a matter of trends and fash-ions that go their own way without the guidance of agenda-controlling in-dividuals. This results in a state of affairs that calls for description on a sta-tistical rather than biographical basis. It is ironic to see the partisans of po-litical correctness in academia condemning philosophy as an elitist discipline at the very moment when philosophy itself has abandoned elit-ism and succeeded in making itself over in a populist reconstruction. American philosophy has now well and truly left "the genteel tradition" behind.

The decline of elitism in American philosophy is illustrated in a graphic way when one considers the production of Ph.D.'s in the departments of high prestige universities. Of the five traditional "ivy league" institutions (Yale, Harvard, Princeton, Columbia, and the University of Pennsylvania) only one (viz. Columbia) currently figures on the roster of North American philosophy departments most productive of Ph.D.'s. From the standpoint of Ph.D. training, the most prominent contribution is made by the big U.S. state universities (Michigan, Minnesota, New York, Texas, and Wiscon-sin), and by the large Catholic institutions. At present the biggest single producer of philosophy Ph.D.'s in North America is the University of To-ronto.

If such a perspective is indeed valid, certain far-reaching implications follow for the eventual historiography of present-day American philoso-phy. For it indicates a situation with which no historian of philosophy has as yet come to terms. In the "heroic" era of the past, the historian of the philosophy of a place and time could safely concentrate upon the *dominant* figures and expect thereby to achieve a certain completeness with respect to "what really mattered". But such an approach is grossly unsuited to the conditions of the present era. For the reality of it is that the "dominant fig-ures" have lost control of the agenda. To accommodate the prevailing reali-ties, the story of present-day American philosophy must be presented in a much more aggregated and statistically articulated format. Treatment by substantial *trends* must replace treatment by dominant individuals, with in-dividuals figuring at best in the role of exemplars. For insofar as single in-dividuals are dealt with as such, it must be done against a vastly enlarged background—they must now be seen as *representative* rather than as *de-terminative* figures, with the status of those individual philosopher selected for historical consideration generally downgraded into a merely exemplary (illustrative) instance of a larger trend.

7. THE DIMINUTION OF PHILOSOPHY NOTWITHSTANDING ITS GROWTH

In the meanwhile, the whole story that is being recounted here with respect to philosophy is being retold at another, higher level of scale and comprehensiveness. For philosophy does not exist in isolation. The size-explosion that has affected it is something that also occurs in the world of learning, science, and culture at large. Just as any given field of philosophy occupies a smaller fraction of the whole, so philosophy at large has become a smaller and less significant and influential fraction of the intellectual domain.

In terms of a geometric analogy, it is clear that if a restricted domain is a subsector of another larger one and—as per the situation of exponential growth—the *rate of increase* of a domain is proportional to its size (so that the larger domain increases faster than the smaller), then of course this smaller (however fast it grows) will be a *proportionally* ever diminishing subsector of the larger. In warrant experience exactly this principle holds for any given branch or problem area of philosophy in relation to the larger whole. But it also holds with respect to the relation of philosophy to the world of learning at large.

And so it becomes only natural to ask: Do American philosophers exert influence? Here, of course, the critical question is: Upon whom? First consider: upon *other philosophers*. We have already remarked that the extent to which even "the leading philosophers" manage to influence others is highly fragmentary—in each case only a small sector of the entire group being involved. Turning now to *the wider society at large*, it must be said that the answer is emphatically negative. American philosophers are not opinion-shapers: they do not have access to the media, to the political establishment, to the "think tanks" that seek to mould public opinion. Insofar as they exert an external influence at all, it is confined to *academics* of other fields. Professors of government may read John Rawls, professors of literature Richard Rorty, professors of linguistics W. V. Quine. But, outside the academy, the writings of such important contemporary American philosophers exert no influence. It was otherwise earlier in the century—in the era of philosophers like William James, John Dewey, and George Santayana—when the writings of individual philosophers set the stage for at least some discussions and debates among a wider public. But it is certainly not so in the America of today. Philosophers (and academics in general) play a very little role in the molding of an "informed public opinion" in the USA—such work is largely done by publicists, film-makers, and talk-show hosts. American society today does not reflect the concerns of philosophers. But to a very large extent the reverse is also the case. By dwelling in the comfortable confines of the Ivory Tower, American philosophers to a large extent repay the nonconcern of society in kind.

8. SUMMARY

The present deliberations have canvassed a series of these six significant phenomena characterizing the status of contemporary American philosophy.

- experiential growth

- agenda enlargement and disciplinary fragmentation

- taxonomic growth/diversification

- attention diffusion

- democratization (decreasing role for a dominant elite)

- inability of a Great Man approach to provide an adequate overall account

What we have here is, in effect, an explanatory cascade: a series of phenomena of such a sort that the reason for being of each item depends on the operation of the aggregate of its predecessors. So we here are confronted not with a set of isolated, randomly conjoined phenomena, but with an integrated process consisting in the coordinated operation of factors joined in a sequentially connected explanatory rationale.

In the end, the upshot of these deliberations is that the quantitative growth of American philosophy in people and publications has transformed the discipline in a way that renders traditional historiographic approaches—with their virtually exclusive focus on prominent individuals—unable to give anything like a faithful account of the discipline at large.

NOTES FOR CHAPTER 12

[1] Such information can be gleaned from the *Directory of American Philosophers*, published by the Philosophy Documentation Center of Charlottesville, Virginia. Observe that these data indicate that in 1990 there were some 40 philosophers per society while in 2000 there were some 90. Professional interaction has accordingly become less intimate in scope.

[2] Of course journals will increase in number more slowly than books. For journals represent entire problem-areas of research, and the Law of Taxonomic Growth has it that the higher an item stands on the scale of taxa, the slower its growth-rate will be. (See N. Rescher, *Epistemetrics*, Cambridge: Cambridge University Press, 2006.)

[3] Any programmatic issue of the *Proceedings and Addresses of the American Philosophical Association* presents a like picture.

[4] *The Encyclopedia of Philosophy*, ed. by Paul Edwards (London and New York: Macmillan, 1967).

[5] John Passmore's *Recent Philosophers* (La Salle, 1985) is perhaps as close as anything we have, but—as the very title indicates—this excellent survey makes no pretensions to comprehensiveness.

[6] The scattershot nature of recent American philosophy is illustrated—among innumerable examples—by the 1970 volume entitled *The Future of Metaphysics* edited by Robert E. Wood (Chicago, Quadrangle Books). Not only are the seventeen contributors disagreed as to the future of metaphysics, they are in substantial dissensus regarding its past as well: what the definitive tasks of the field are, which practitioners afford the best role-models, and which approaches have proved to be the most promising.

[7] This already became apparent in the 1960s. See *TIME Magazine, Time* Essay: "What (If Anything) to Expect from Today's Philosophers," vol. 87 (January 7, 1966), pp. 24-25.

[8] Data from Carnegie Foundation for the Advancement of Teaching, entitled *Carnegie Survey of Undergraduates, 1986*, as reported in *The Chronicle of Higher Education*, Feb. 5, 1986, pp. 27-30.

[9] This phenomenon, which occurs not just in philosophy but pervasively throughout academic publication, has become known as *quality retardation*. On this phenomenon see Nicholas Rescher, *Epistemetrics* (Cambridge: Cambridge University Press, 2006).

NOTES FOR CHAPTER 12

[10] The process at issue relates to the principle known in the social sciences as Rousseau's Law, maintaining that in a population of size n the number of high-visibility members stands as the square root of n. Thus in a profession of 10,000 we would expect to find some 100 widely recognized contributors.)

[11] Where Ortega himself did not expect it: "Philosophy needs no protection, no attention, no sympathy, no interest in the part of the masses. Its perfect uselessness protects it." (*The Revolt of the Masses* tr. by Anthony Kerrigan [Notre Dame: University of Notre Dame Press, 1989], p. 73.) Ortega did not reckon with "applied philosophy".

[12] As long ago as the 1960s the General Editor of a first-rate survey of American humanistic scholarship wrote in the Foreword to the volume on philosophy: "Not many of the names mentioned in these pages are recognizable as those of great intellectual leaders, and many are unknown even to an old academic hand like myself who has a fair speaking acquaintance with the various humanistic disciplines in America." (Richard Schlatter in Roderick Chisholm et. al., *Philosophy: Princeton Studies of Humanistic Scholarship in America* (Englewood Cliffs: Prentice Hall, 1964.), p. x. This situation would be even more pronounced today.

NAME INDEX

Nicholas Rescher

Collected Paper. 14 Volumes

Nicholas Rescher is University Professor of Philosophy at the University of Pittsburgh where he also served for many years as Director of the *Center for Philosophy of Science*. He is a former president of the Eastern Division of the *American Philosophical Association*, and has also served as President of the *American Catholic Philosophical Association*, the *American Metaphysical Society*, the *American G. W. Leibniz Society*, and the *C. S. Peirce Society*. An honorary member of *Corpus Christi College*, Oxford, he has been elected to membership in the *European Academy of Arts and Sciences* (Academia Europaea), the *Institut International de Philosophie*, and several other learned academies. Having held visiting lectureships at Oxford, Constance, Salamanca, Munich, and Marburg, Professor Rescher has received seven honorary degrees from universities on three continents (2006 at the University of Helsinki). Author of some hundred books ranging over many areas of philosophy, over a dozen of them translated into other languages, he was awarded the Alexander von Humboldt Prize for Humanistic Scholarship in 1984.

ontos verlag has published a series of collected papers of Nicholas Rescher in three parts with altogether fourteen volumes, each of which will contain roughly ten chapters/essays (some new and some previously published in scholarly journals). The fourteen volumes would cover the following range of topics:

Volumes I - XIV

STUDIES IN 20TH CENTURY PHILOSOPHY
ISBN 3-937202-78-1 · 215 pp. Hardcover, EUR 75,00

STUDIES IN PRAGMATISM
ISBN 3-937202-79-X · 178 pp. Hardcover, EUR 69,00

STUDIES IN IDEALISM
ISBN 3-937202-80-3 · 191 pp. Hardcover, EUR 69,00

STUDIES IN PHILOSOPHICAL INQUIRY
ISBN 3-937202-81-1 · 206 pp. Hardcover, EUR 79,00

STUDIES IN COGNITIVE FINITUDE
ISBN 3-938793-00-7 . 118 pp. Hardcover, EUR 69,00

STUDIES IN SOCIAL PHILOSOPHY
ISBN 3-938793-01-5 . 195 pp. Hardcover, EUR 79,00

STUDIES IN PHILOSOPHICAL ANTHROPOLOGY
ISBN 3-938793-02-3 . 165 pp. Hardcover, EUR 79,00

STUDIES IN VALUE THEORY
ISBN 3-938793-03-1 . 176 pp. Hardcover, EUR 79,00

STUDIES IN METAPHILOSOPHY
ISBN 3-938793-04-X . 221 pp. Hardcover, EUR 79,00

STUDIES IN THE HISTORY OF LOGIC
ISBN 3-938793-19-8 . 178 pp. Hardcover, EUR 69,00

STUDIES IN THE PHILOSOPHY OF SCIENCE
ISBN 3-938793-20-1 . 273 pp. Hardcover, EUR 79,00

STUDIES IN METAPHYSICAL OPTIMALISM
ISBN 3-938793-21-X . 96 pp. Hardcover, EUR 49,00

STUDIES IN LEIBNIZ'S COSMOLOGY
ISBN 3-938793-22-8 . 229 pp. Hardcover, EUR 69,00

STUDIES IN EPISTEMOLOGY
ISBN 3-938793-23-6 . 180 pp. Hardcover, EUR 69,00

ontos verlag

Frankfurt • Paris • Lancaster • New Brunswick

2006. 14 Volumes, Approx. 2630 pages.
Format 14,8 x 21 cm
Hardcover **EUR 798,00**
ISBN 10: 3-938793-25-2
Due October 2006

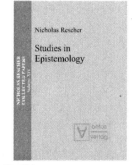

P.O. Box 1541 • D-63133 Heusenstamm bei Frankfurt
www.ontosverlag.com • info@ontosverlag.com
Tel. ++49-6104-66 57 33 • Fax ++49-6104-66 57 34